Bumped Up

Pam Greer

Published by Lechner Syndications

www.lechnersyndications.com

Copyright © 2014 Pam Greer

ISBN 13: 978-1-927794-18-0

"Sports like volleyball do not build character, they reveal it."

~Anonymous

CONTENTS

CHAPTER 1

Victory for Hickory Academy was close. From the bench, Neeka Leigh watched as the girls from her basketball team soared down the court toward the opposing team's defenses. Hickory Academy had just scored, but halfway down the court, Payton, the star of the team and Neeka's best friend, had intercepted a pass. Now they were back in enemy territory, grins upon their faces. It never took long for Payton to score.

Neeka studied her friend carefully. Payton Moore was super tall with toned muscles and an agility rarely seen in a fourteen-year-old. She was a dominating force on the court. She glided around gracefully, half wolf, half ballerina. She admired her friend's athleticism. Though Neeka pushed herself hard, shooting hoops outside almost every night before bed, she still could never match Payton when it came to natural talent. That's why she was on the bench and Payton was out in the spotlight.

"I'm open," Neeka heard Selina Cho yell.

But Payton had a clean shot. Effortlessly, she drove the ball into the hoop, adding to an already massive lead over the competition.

Selina scowled momentarily, but quickly recovered, her brown eyes smug as the scoreboard changed. To Selina, winning was more important than anything else, including pride.

The Hickory Academy JV basketball team was hosting the last

scrimmage of basketball camp at their school. Technically, she and Payton weren't on the team yet. They'd still have to try out at the end of October, but as entering freshmen who had played for Hickory Academy Middle School, they'd been invited to join the JV team at camp.

Neeka wasn't worried by the fact she was sitting on the bench. Though she didn't consider herself a great player, she knew that with practice and hard work, she'd eventually improve. It was worth the effort. Payton was like a sister to her. The time they shared playing basketball together was a lot of fun. She loved it, even if it meant playing in Payton's shadow.

Jamari, her brother, didn't understand it. A celebrated high school basketball player himself, he often joked that Neeka was the only black girl who couldn't play basketball, to which she would reply by flicking him across the head and protesting that she couldn't help it that she was only five foot three.

Neeka searched the bleachers for Jamari. He sat near the top. Payton's mother and her own mom sat next to him. Sadly, both of their fathers were missing. Her dad was at work. He worked as a nurse, a career that involved long, tiring hours. Payton's dad had recently moved to Cincinnati and couldn't make it down for the scrimmage. It was strange not seeing Mr. Moore in the bleachers. Up until a year ago, Brandon was like a coach to Payton, offering his support and advice at nearly every game they played. Neeka knew his absence was difficult for her friend.

At least Payton had Neeka's family to help fill the void of her missing dad. Kind of. Both their moms were caught up in a conversation that clearly had nothing to do with basketball, but Jamari was paying attention. He gave his sister a thumbs up.

Sometimes, Neeka wished Jamari would be hauled off to another planet by aliens, but when they weren't fighting, they were actually really close. She would miss him when she started high school. More than ever, she wished they'd be attending the same school. He was going to be a junior, but he attended a magnet school on the other side of Nashville. The brainiac. How the boy could be such a smarty pants but still walk down to breakfast wearing his shirt inside out was beyond her.

They had plans to spend the last months of summer at their grandma's house in Georgia. Staying with Memaw was always a treat. Their visit promised peach pies and plenty of Coke. Mostly, they spent their days swimming in the lake, playing board games underneath the air-conditioning unit, and picking peaches at the orchard near Memaw's house. Neeka would trade Jamari for a slice of peach pie right now if she could. She was starving.

As she turned her attention away from her family and back toward the basketball game, a surprising sight caught her eye. Annette Reynolds sat in the bleachers, along with the rest of the varsity volleyball team at Hickory Academy. Neeka recognized Annette, the team captain, from sports open day the high school had hosted at the end of the previous school year for entering freshmen. It's where she and Payton had registered their interest in the basketball program. The volleyball table had been nearby. The basketball table had been crowded, but the space surrounding the volleyball table had been mostly empty. Volleyball was a new sport at Hickory Academy. Neeka remembered how Annette had stared down the large group of basketball players, an intensity upon her face that was almost scary.

What's the varsity volleyball team doing at a JV basketball scrimmage? Neeka wondered.

Annette tightened the ponytail that kept her wavy brown hair pulled back, then pointed down at the court, directly at Payton. She turned to whisper to the other volleyball players. Neeka couldn't hear their conversation, but Annette was obviously enthusiastic about something.

Neeka tried to call upon the Force to lip-read their conversation, but her plan was interrupted when their coach called a time out.

"Leigh, you're in!" she shouted.

Finally! Neeka thought, jumping up and warming her muscles, shaking away any stiffness from sitting out most of the game.

She was replacing Selina. "Don't drop the ball," Selina quipped as she sat on the bench. Even though Selina insisted on a short tomboy haircut, she was pretty. Being of Korean decent, she had delicate features, which she usually kept hidden behind a constant smirk.

"Try not to scare away the boys with all that mascara running down

3

your face. Talk about sweaty," Neeka retorted.

Selina grinned, enjoying the challenge. "Thatta girl, Neeka. Now put that fight into the game," she hollered as Neeka stepped onto the court.

"Ready to rumble?" Payton asked, winking at her friend.

"Girl, you know it," Neeka said with determination.

Neeka was revved up, but she knew her presence would neither help nor hurt the game. Hickory Academy had too great of a lead, thanks to Payton.

Before the whistle blew to officially restart the game, Neeka looked into the bleachers again. Sure enough, Annette and the rest of the volleyball girls were still focused on Payton.

Neeka wondered what they wanted.

****

"Do you want to sleep over at my place on Saturday, before you go to your grandma's house?" Payton mumbled, still wearing her mouth guard.

As expected, Hickory Academy had won the scrimmage. The opposing team had left, shaking in their sneakers. The wrath of the Hickory Academy JV team would certainly circulate. They'd be unstoppable come November.

Neeka zipped up her equipment bag and set it on the bench, waiting for Payton to finish packing up. "Definitely. I can't leave without one last sleepover. We *have* to watch that new Selana Gomez movie."

Payton frowned and spit out her mouth guard. "Neeka, what am I going to do while you're away at your grandma's? I'm going to miss you."

Neeka remembered when she first met Payton. She'd started attending Hickory Academy in fourth grade. Though she was still only a young kid at the time, in a private school like Hickory Academy, where most of its pupils filtered through its adjacent campuses from kindergarten to high school, fourth grade was a late year to start. Most of the kids already knew each other well. They accepted her warmly enough, but she never really felt as though she fit in.

The next year, Payton started at Hickory Academy. Neeka was no longer the new girl, which she was thankful for. Identifying with Payton, Neeka sat next to her at lunch on the first day of class and started up a conversation with the quiet, tall girl.

"I'm Neeka," she had said, handing Payton a sticker with a glittering yellow star.

Payton thanked her for the gift. "You have a cool name."

"It's short for Renika. My mom wanted something that sounded like "unique." Unfortunately, now all my brother calls me is Neeka the Stinka. But don't tell anyone that."

"What's your brother's name?"

"Jamari."

Payton thought for a minute. "Maybe you should start calling him Jamari the Sorry."

From that moment on, Payton was one of Neeka's favorite people. Soon, Payton asked her if she wanted to join her at the Y for fifth grade basketball. Basketball practices turned to sleepovers, and the girls had been inseparable ever since.

"I'll call you every night," Neeka promised, trying to cheer her friend up as Payton took off her basketball sneakers to put on a pair of sandals. She knew she would call. Her grandma's house in Georgia was large and creaky. It scared her. She always called Payton at night before going to bed. It helped her to sleep.

Payton still looked sad.

"We're going to miss you next year," Valerie Sutton said, approaching them from the bleachers. She and a few of the teammates they were leaving behind at Hickory Academy Middle School had come to watch the scrimmage. She was replacing Payton as captain.

"Don't worry, you'll be joining us next year," Payton said. "Then it'll be like having the old team back."

"Yeah, but next year I won't be captain," Valerie said casually, then walked away.

"That was odd," Neeka said. She was never really sure how she felt about Valerie. The girl was nice enough, but her loyalties wavered. Neeka didn't believe she was totally trustworthy.

Oh well, it'll be another year before I have to deal with Val again, she thought.

Neeka helped Payton gather the rest of her gear. She was still hungry and wanted to hurry home to dinner. Her mom had mentioned something about pizza. But as they approached the doors to the back exit where they knew their moms were waiting outside, Annette and the varsity volleyball girls intentionally blocked their path.

Annette had her arms crossed. "We want to talk to you, Payton." It was less of a request and more of a demand.

"Hi." A girl with sandy blonde hair and blue eyes greeted them, trying to make up for Annette's rudeness. Though the girl was fair, she looked as if she had a bit of Latina blood in her. "I'm Lacey Knox, a member of the varsity volleyball team at Hickory Academy. We'd like to talk to Payton."

Annette stepped forward, making her position as leader clear. Lacey backed down. "You've got skills, girl. I'm impressed."

Though Payton was taller than Annette, the senior had a commanding presence. Even with badly sunburnt skin and freckles, she had the authority of a warrior queen. Neeka stood a little bit straighter, trying to elongate her body, imitating Annette's posture.

Ignoring Neeka completely, Annette moved closer to Payton. "Trust me, I'm not easy to impress."

"Thanks," Payton said shyly, clearly intimidated by the older girl.

Payton was always too concerned about what people thought. Neeka hated to say it, but Payton was a people pleaser. On the court, she was a bulldozer. Off the court, she was polite as a puppy.

"What exactly do you want?" Neeka demanded on behalf of her friend.

Annette continued to ignore her. "As you may know, Payton, the Hickory Academy volleyball team is entering their third year. We're good, but not good enough. I want us to be the best. I want this team to go to the District Championships and win. With your height and footwork, you'd be the perfect hitter and blocker to get us there. I want you on my team, Payton." Again, it sounded like a demand.

"Please join us," Lacey pleaded.

Neeka couldn't believe what she was hearing. The girls wanted Payton to play varsity volleyball! It was rare that a freshman ever got to be on a varsity team. She was so happy for Payton. This was so exciting!

"I have to ask my parents first, but I'm sure it'll be okay," Payton said. She was trying to play cool, but Neeka could tell her friend was jumping up and down inside.

"Good. Volleyball camp is the first week of August. Be prepared," Annette ordered.

The varsity girls turned to leave, but as Annette walked away, she stopped and added, "Don't make me regret putting a freshman on my team, Payton."

"I won't," Payton stammered.

That was uncalled for, Neeka thought.

As soon as the other girls were through the doors, Neeka and Payton turned to each other. "Oh my God!" the squealed together in unison.

"High school, here we come!" Neeka shouted eagerly.

CHAPTER 2

I'm going to play on the varsity volleyball team!

Payton still couldn't believe it. She was used to being the best. She had a million trophies in her room, from basketball to tennis. There were so many, her mom wanted to put some of the trophies into storage, but Payton refused. Though she was used to winning championships and being captain, making the varsity volleyball team while only a freshman—that was a whole new achievement!

Prancing into her room, Payton flopped down on her bedspread— navy and light blue, the same color as the Titans football team—and squealed with excitement.

She hadn't even walked into her first class yet, and already high school promised to be full of exciting new beginnings.

But as she relived in her mind the moment Annette recruited her onto the varsity team, another feeling came over Payton, one she was not used to.

Doubt.

Payton quickly shook the feeling away. She was a top athlete. It didn't matter that she'd never played volleyball at a competitive level before. She was strong and she was quick. No matter what, she'd make sure Hickory Academy was the District Champion this year.

Still, she suddenly wished her dad were there. He'd been her personal coach all these years. "Never settle for silver," he'd tell her.

"You're only the best if you're standing on the top podium." He understood her drive to win.

Payton never told her mom this, only Neeka, but the real reason she refused to put her trophies into storage was because they reminded her of all the moments she'd shared with her dad. While she was winning medals and breaking records, he was always by her side. Without him there, she felt a little lost.

Quickly, she reached over to the hot-dog-shaped phone by the side of her bed and called her dad. He answered by the fourth ring. He always did. Since moving to Cincinnati, he never missed her calls. He had a special ringtone for her on his phone. It was "Brown Eyed Girl" by some old guy whose name she couldn't remember. Van something or other. She didn't know why that was her ringtone. Her eyes were green. But her dad was funny like that.

"Hey baby girl, you're a sight for sore eyes."

"Dad, you can't see me." Payton laughed.

"You know what I mean. How are you?"

He sounded happy and relaxed. Payton was glad. She didn't know much about marriage, but she did know that this separation had stressed her dad out and given him a few extra gray hairs.

"You'll never believe what happened. I was at basketball camp and there were these girls from the volleyball team scouting for new players. And they chose me!"

"Hickory Academy has a volleyball team?" he asked uncertainly.

"DAD! What part of 'they chose me' did you not understand? I'm going to play varsity my freshman year!"

Payton could almost hear him sit up in his seat. "That's great news, baby girl!" he exclaimed. "I always said you were a winner."

Twirling the phone cord around her finger, Payton tried to choose her next words carefully. "You don't think you can come down for a few weeks and help me practice before volleyball camp, do you?"

Her dad hesitated. "You know nothing would make me happier, but I don't think I can take the time off work. I just started this job. Someone has to pay for your college education."

"That's years away, Daddy. Plus, I'll just get an athletic scholarship." Though she argued, she knew his answer would still be a reluctant "no."

"Then you won't mind if I go ahead and spend the savings I put aside for you on new golf clubs?" he joked.

"Daddy!" Payton laughed. "Don't you dare."

"I suppose I'll continue saving it for a rainy college day. Just don't grow up too fast, baby girl."

"I'll try not to," Payton said. "I guess I'll let you get back to work."

"That's my superstar. Now go and make Daddy proud at volleyball camp."

"I will," Payton promised before hanging up.

****

The sporting store in the mall near her house was one of Payton's favorite places in the whole world. She imagined that what she felt when she was in the store was what astronauts felt like when they were in space. Everything about the store lifted her mood, from the smell of new equipment to the funky, colorful sneakers they had on display in the shoe department.

"The lighting in this place is horrible," her mom grumbled with disgust. "And the carpet is way too dark for such an open space."

Payton rolled her eyes. Her mom was an interior designer and had a habit of criticizing every store they went into. "The kneepads are just over there," she said, pointing to the back corner of the giant warehouse.

Her mom, Allison, followed her, sighing as she tugged at her short brown hair. "I still don't understand why you can't just wear your soccer kneepads to volleyball camp. I mean, a kneepad is a kneepad."

"They're totally different," Payton insisted. "For starters, we wear shin guards in soccer, not kneepads. You know, those things that cover my shins, not my knees?"

Her mom was unimpressed. "And the shoes?" she asked as they moved past the swimwear section. "In volleyball, you run on a court.

And in basketball, you run on a court. I don't understand why you need different shoes."

"Volleyball shoes are lighter so you can jump easier, okay? My teammates are counting on me. I need the best equipment so I can be the best."

Her mom huffed. "You sound like your father."

"I don't think that's a bad thing," Payton snapped. She was growing frustrated with her mom's lack of understanding.

"It still just doesn't make sense to me, Payton. Why didn't you have to try out for the team? I've never heard of a varsity team not holding try-outs before."

It took all of Payton's willpower not to scream out of annoyance. Why did her mom have to ask so many questions? She wished her dad were here. When he was around, her mom didn't wonder about things so much, like why they had to buy new kneepads and shoes.

"They did have try-outs," Payton explained for what felt like the hundredth time. "But it's only their third season. They just don't have enough players on the team. You can't play unless you have enough players to fill every position. They needed a hitter, so they asked me to join, along with a few other girls. Simple as." Payton didn't mean to, but she heard the anger in her voice.

Her mom stopped walking and gently set her hand on Payton's shoulder. "I'm sorry. You know how proud I am of you, sweetie. Choose whatever kneepads you want."

"Thanks," Payton said, grateful for the offer. "I really do want to bring the varsity team to the District Championships."

"I know," said her mom.

Though Payton was glad her mom was finally listening, she knew she still didn't understand. If her dad were there, he'd be coaching her every morning and every evening, preparing her for the challenge ahead. The best her mom could do was nod and pretend she knew what it was like to have a fire burning in your stomach, one that wouldn't stop until glory was brought to your team.

As she searched through the kneepads for the best brand she could find, she knew that if their shopping trip that afternoon proved one thing, it was that Payton didn't want to do this alone.

* * * * * * * * * * * * * * * * * * *

"Please, please, please," Payton pleaded into the phone. "I need you. You know what I mean, jelly bean?"

Neeka laughed. "Payton, I'm not sure my parents will let me attend volleyball camp. They've just paid for our basketball camp. Plus, Jamari and I are supposed to go to Memaw's for a few weeks before school starts, remember?"

"But you were just at your grandma's house last month," Payton whined. "I really need you, Neeka. Please say you'll join the JV team. Think about how much fun we'll have playing basketball. Now we can double that fun by playing volleyball together too!"

"But you're on the varsity team."

"Didn't I tell you? When Annette called to give me all the details for volleyball camp, she said I'd be playing for both the JV and varsity teams. The JV team is a bit low on numbers as well, but none of the varsity girls are willing to play both. Since I'm a freshman, it's my obligation. That's what Annette said. So you see, Neeka, the JV team needs you."

"I doubt I'm the one they need..."

Though Neeka was resisting, Payton knew she could convince her to join. She could hear the eagerness in her best friend's voice. Neeka had never been afraid to take on an activity she wasn't perfect at, and Payton knew the idea of attending another summer camp together was too good for her friend to refuse.

"I'll have to ask..." Neeka said, faltering.

"Do more than ask. Insist!" Payton said, jumping up on her bed, the cell phone tucked snuggly under her chin. "We can bring our pink super soakers to camp and start another water fight."

"No! We were nearly kicked off the basketball team for doing that last year," Neeka reminded her, giggling into the phone.

"Get Jamari on your side. Tell him playing volleyball will help you improve your lateral movements in basketball."

"I don't think Jamari can even say 'lateral,'" Neeka teased.

"Ya just lost me as captain of team PR," Jamari yelled from somewhere in the background.

"Is he playing video games?" Payton asked.

"Is he ever not playing video games?"

They both laughed.

"I promise I'll ask my parents tonight when they get home from their dinner date."

Payton clapped her hands in excitement, nearly dropping the phone as she did so. "Great! I know your dad will be okay with it. It's your mom I'm worried about. She'll probably try to say you'll exhaust yourself playing two sports, even though basketball doesn't start until volleyball finishes. There's very little overlap."

"That's exactly what she'll say," Neeka said loudly. "And she'll worry about my grades."

Payton considered this. "Then take out your report cards from seventh grade. Remind her that was the year you also took on gymnastics, but you still got high grades. She can't argue with that."

"No, but she can bring up how I fell off the balance beam and sprained my ankle, thus ending my life in gymnastics."

Someone started laughing in the background. It could only be Jamari. Sure enough, Payton soon heard him say, "That was hilarious! I really need to upload that video onto YouTube."

"No one wants to see a poor little girl fall," Neeka snapped. "But they might want to see a junior in high school get beaten down by his little sister!"

Before meeting Neeka, Payton would pray for a brother or sister. But now she had one of each. They were her adopted siblings. At times, she wished she lived in the Leigh household, especially now that her dad had moved out.

"I'll call you after I ask my parents. But first, I have to stop a certain bumble brain from hacking into my computer to steal my gymnastic videos," Neeka grumbled. "TTYL."

****

It felt like hours before Neeka called her back. When her cell phone began to play Call Me Maybe, Payton nervously picked up the phone, afraid of what her friend's answer would be. She hadn't admitted to Neeka how insecure she felt without her dad there or how much she really needed a friend to support her on her journey—someone to fill the role of confidante that her dad would have played.

"So I have bad news," Neeka said as soon as Payton answered.

Payton felt her heart drop. She couldn't do this without Neeka. She really needed her friend there.

Neeka continued. "Mom says we'll have to buy my volleyball equipment at a thrift store, in case I sprain my ankle blocking the ball."

Confused, Payton took a minute to register what her friend was saying. "Wait…"

"I'm joining the JV team!" Neeka shouted giddily into the phone. "We can now add volleyball sisters to our list!"

"This is going to be so much fun," Payton squeaked.

"So what now? Do I have to register somewhere?"

Payton ran to her desk and flipped through the printout of the information sheet Annette had emailed her. "I have the number for the JV coach here. Her name is Coach Gina. Call her and let her know you'll be on the team." She read out the number while Neeka wrote it down.

"Are there try-outs?" Neeka asked, though Payton could hear Mrs. Leigh whispering the questions to her daughter.

"No. The numbers are too small to hold try-outs."

"Do I have to wear those horrible—" Neeka stopped. "Mom, I'm not going to ask that. I like the shorts." Payton heard a hand cover the phone, muting whatever Neeka's mother was saying, but Payton could still hear Neeka's reply. "It's not about attracting the boys, mom. The shorts have to be that short to move easily around the court… No! I will NOT wear my basketball shorts instead of volleyball shorts."

Payton went to her closet to choose her pajamas, humming along to a song she'd heard earlier on the radio as she stretched the cord of her phone, keeping the cell phone firmly beneath her ear. This conversation could take a while. Mrs. Leigh was strict about her daughter's modesty, especially since they had entered their teens, but Payton also knew Lawanda would give in eventually, only because it was for an athletic pursuit.

"Tell her it's like wearing a swimsuit on the swim team," Payton volunteered.

"Good one," Neeka whispered. She returned a minute later. "It worked. Mom was on the swim team in high school. She's going to call Coach Gina tomorrow."

"What are you going to do about your grandma's?" "Camp is only two weeks away. We'll go after."

"You sure you can wait that long for peach pie?"

Neeka laughed. "For you, Payton, I'd give up peach pie completely."

CHAPTER 3

A huge banner with the motto "Serve Your Team" glistened in the morning sun above the doors leading into the gymnasium of a giant community center in the downtown area of Nashville, not too far from Hickory Academy. The center was brand new, with a stone exterior and floor-to-ceiling windows. It felt like a place where top athletes trained. Clean and modern. With her equipment bag slung across her shoulder, Payton stood on a curb just outside, waiting anxiously for Neeka to arrive. She was roasting. Thank goodness they'd be spending most of the next four days in the air-conditioned gym.

Her mother had dropped her off earlier before rushing to a beauty appointment. "I hope you don't mind, sweetie, but mommy has had this appointment booked for months, way before you even knew you'd be playing volleyball. You'll understand when you're older."

"Why are you talking to me like I'm five?" had been Payton's reply.

As teams full of girls with bouncy ponytails and personalized volleyball gear hoarded past her to enter the gym, she began to wonder if she made a mistake. This was unknown territory. Usually, she would have her dad with her. He would have been coaching her from the moment Annette recruited her. Payton would have walked into camp already a star in the making.

Suddenly, a silver jeep blared its horn as it sped into the parking lot and stopped right in front of Payton.

"How ya doing?" Jamari asked from the driver's side window.

"Some heat, huh?"

"If you haven't noticed, my brother has no perception of speed when driving," Neeka said irritably as she unbuckled her seatbelt. "I blame his big ole Hobbit feet."

Jamari looked down at his sandals as he stepped out of the jeep and reached for Neeka's bags in the back. "They're not so big."

Neeka joined him. "No, but they are clumsy and hairy."

"What do hairy feet have to do with speed?"

"It's dangerous, that's all I'm saying. Geesh, Jamari, do you not think of everyone else on the roads? Kids play on these streets."

Looking slightly embarrassed, Jamari's only reply was, "What'cha got in this bag? Oh wait, let me guess, you bought out all the rolls of toilet paper in Nashville so you have enough to cushion your fall every time you land on your face."

Neeka flicked him across the head. "I'm not going to fall on my face," she protested.

"She's going to be great," Payton added. "Anyway, we're just here to have fun."

"Didn't you say that in fifth grade when you both signed up to play basketball at the Y? Years later, and Neeka the Stinka still comes home with bumps and bruises after practice."

"You're one to talk," Neeka pouted. "Didn't you come home with a black eye after the Regional Tournament last year?"

"That's different. My black eye came in battle. Yours are from falling over your own two feet. Who's the Hobbit now?" Jamari laughed at his own joke.

Neeka grabbed her bag roughly out of his hands. "You know what the best thing about volleyball camp is? Four days without you around."

Jamari opened his arms wide. "Come on, sis, you know you love me."

"The way a cat loves a thorn in its foot," Neeka huffed, but smiled.

"Sis, don't keep me waiting. You know I'll stand here all day."

Reluctantly, Neeka smiled and gave her brother a long hug.

"Payton," Jamari said, peeking over the top of his sister's head. "What are you waiting for, adopted sis?"

Smiling, Payton joined in on the hug too. It helped to calm her nerves.

Then Jamari finally drove off, slower than when he drove in.

"This is so exciting," Payton said. "But my tummy feels like there's a whole bunch of butterflies fluttering around."

"I'm nervous too," Neeka admitted. "But if we work hard, I'm sure we'll pick it up in no time. Remember, we've played volleyball before."

"Yeah, but that was in PE class where our grade was based on attendance alone. I don't think half of us knew what we were doing. Here, we're expected to actually be good at what we do. I have a feeling today is going to be a long day."

I wish my dad was here, she thought forlornly.

Neeka reached into one of her bags. "This won't help the nerves, but if you're hungry, I have granola bars."

Payton shook her head. "No thanks. I had buttermilk biscuits and sausage gravy for breakfast."

"Yeah, mom made me eat an entire omelet before she went off to work this morning."

"You girls heading inside, or you just gonna talk about grits and gravy all morning?" Lacey asked playfully, coming out up behind them. She carried a large box of T-shirts.

"Those ours?" Payton asked, peeking into the box. The T-shirts were blue with green and white detailing—the Hickory Academy colors.

Lacey adjusted the box. "Yep, but just for camp. We'll get our jerseys at the official start of the season." Her eyes flashed. "Camp is so exciting, isn't it? We had so much fun last year. I'm glad volleyball season is finally here again. But it's also kinda sad. I'm a junior, but many of the varsity girls are graduating this year. This will be our last camp with a lot of them."

"Then let's make it a season they'll never forget," Neeka said. "For both the JV and varsity teams."

Lacey nodded in agreement.

Saying nothing, Payton followed the other two girls into the gymnasium, glancing one last time at the banner above the door.

Serve Your Team.

****

The gymnasium was crowded with players, parents, and coaches from a dozen or so schools. A spectrum of colored T-shirts filtered around the room, from neon orange to navy blue to metallic pink. Large banners with volleyball emblems advertised local sponsors and signified where coaches were to sign their teams in, accompanied by the camp instructors, most college-level players on loan from the local universities. A professional videographer zigzagged around the room, capturing the opening moments of camp.

Though a few players were pulling stunts with the balls, no one was formally warming up yet. Payton was slightly relieved. She was still trying to calm her nerves.

The Hickory Academy team was in the far corner. As they moved closer to their team, Payton spotted a man with spiky blonde hair and analytical brown eyes towered over them, occasionally calling out something from his clipboard. She assumed it was Coach Michael Ross, the head of the Hickory Academy volleyball program and coach to the varsity team. Dressed in a blue polo shirt and khaki shorts, he stood rigidly as if he was commanding an army, but something about his demeanor told Payton that the effect was for coaching purposes only. Maybe it was the slight hint of a grin that threatened the corner of his lips, as though he was as amused as he was stern. Or maybe it was the Tweety Bird tattoo on his bicep.

Standing nearby was a woman with black curly hair and sunglasses on the top of her head. Her light blue eyes admired the players appreciatively. She wore fashionable denim shorts and a T-shirt that matched the ones in the box Lacey carried. Like Coach Mike, she had a volleyball-shaped whistle around her neck. Coach Gina Williams—assistant to Coach Mike.

"That's Coach Gina," Neeka said, matching Payton's thoughts. "My new tormentor."

Payton watched as the woman's face lit up in a big toothy grin while she clapped her hands together in delight at something one of the JV girls had said. "She doesn't seem like the tormentor type to me."

A familiar face grabbed her attention. She pointed. "Look, Selina is here! I didn't know she was joining."

"Looks like I can leave now," Neeka joked.

Payton grabbed her arm tight. "No way, jelly bean. You're not leaving my side."

"Look who I found outside," Lacey said, announcing their arrival to the group. "This is Payton Moore and Neeka Leigh."

Coach Gina bounded toward them. "Welcome, girls," she said warmly.

"Payton, Neeka, hi!" Selina waved from her spot on the floor.

Annette smiled at Payton. "Glad you finally made it to the party, champ," she greeted.

Coach Mike looked up briefly from his clipboard, then returned to whatever it was he was doing.

Lacey set the box she was carrying down. "Now who wants a T-shirt?" The JV girls rushed at her hungrily. The varsity girls waited in the background, playing it cool. Lacey started throwing the T-shirts out in fistfuls. "Congratulations, you all are now part of the Hickory Academy volleyball team."

****

The morning flew by. Before she knew it, Payton, wearing her new T-shirt and volleyball shorts, found herself standing in front of Annette. The senior went over some basic skills with Selina, Neeka, and her. The rest of the JV girls were doing drills alongside the varsity team. They had some minor experience playing volleyball, either as sophomores who had played JV last year but hadn't made the varsity team or as freshmen who had played for church and local teams, since Hickory Academy Middle School had yet to adopt a volleyball program.

"Listen up, newbies," Annette said. "The three of you are pretty good basketball players." She paused, looking at Neeka. "Well, two of you are, anyway. So you know how to move on the court." She picked up a ball and spun it around her hand. "But this is a whole new ball game." She put the ball down.

"Volleyball is a lot more choreographed than basketball. Before the ball is even touched by the other team, you have to be ready. We're allowed just three moves to get the ball over the net, so those moves have to be exact. Those three moves are usually the pass, the set, and the spike," she counted on her fingers.

"Now, because the ball is usually approaching your side of the court fast and hard, you want to be in a ready position—bent knees with your weight on your toes." She imitated the ready position. "A pass, also called a bump, is performed by straightening the arms forward and locking your fists together. How your arms and fists line up is called your platform. Don't run around with your arms stretched out like some crazed zombie. Wait until you're in position before you form your platform. Then pass the ball by letting it bounce off the center of your forearms, somewhere between your inner elbows and your wrists." Annette trailed her finger along her forearm as she talked. "Got it?"

Payton nodded, followed by the other girls.

"Good. You'll practice it later with the team. I want to demonstrate first." Annette relaxed her arms, preparing to skip ahead to the next move. "Whoever gets to the ball first passes it on to the setter."

Selina reluctantly raised her hand.

"What is this, kindergarten?" Annette scoffed.

It feels like it, Payton thought.

"What if two people go for the ball?"

"That won't happen. Volleyball is all about communication. I can't stress that enough. In this game, you have to talk. If you know you have the best chance of successfully passing the ball to the setter, you yell 'Mine!' before you go for it. Let me hear you all yell it."

"Mine?" Selina squeaked, but it sounded more like a question.

Neeka and Payton looked at each other.

Annette was not amused. "If you want to be anywhere near the court today, I expect you to shout 'Mine' before I finish this sentence—"

"Mine!" they all shouted.

"Better. Do it again. And again," Annette instructed.

"Mine!"

"Mine!"

"Mine!"

Their shouts made Payton think of a popular cartoon involving a lost fish and seagulls.

They continued shouting until Coach Mike signaled for Annette to make them stop. "Now you have it," she said. "The cause of most major errors in volleyball is a breakdown in communication. Don't forget it." She paused, taking a sip of water from her sports bottle.

"So, the ball is passed to the setter, who positions the ball for a hitter to send across the net. You do not set the ball using a platform. You bring your hands just above your forehead, palms facing outward, and set the ball to a hitter by extending your arms out, as if you were a superhero about to fly." The serious look on Annette's face after such a silly comparison made the girls giggle, but she ignored them. "The ball is pushed high into the air, giving the hitter time to approach the ball and strike it over."

"I have a question," Payton declared, glad she'd done some homework prior to camp. "I know only six people are allowed to play a side of the court at a time—three in the front row and three in the back row. When it's a team's turn to serve again, everyone rotates clockwise. What is the setter supposed to do then? Do they still set, even if they're in the back row?"

"Yes. Even though you move physical positions, your role essentially stays the same. After the ball goes over the net after a serve, you are allowed to move around the court, meaning the setter can move forward into their setting position, closer to the net."

"Is it the same for the hitters?" Selina asked.

"It's a bit more technical than this, but essentially anyone in the back row can move forward to pass or set the ball, but they cannot attack or hit the ball across the net unless they are standing behind the attack line, also known as the ten-foot line."

The attack line, Payton knew, was a line drawn ten feet away from the net on each side of the court to separate the front-row players from the back-row players.

Annette turned her attention fully to Payton. "There are ways to play defense in volleyball. The main one is called blocking. When the other team is about to strike the ball, a blocker shuffles to where they need to be then springs from their ready position, jumping high in their air with their arms stretched straight up, as if they just won the lottery, and their hands facing toward the middle of the court. Most players shrug their shoulders to help their arms reach their full height. It's important to be close to the net, but not close enough to touch it, even by accident."

"Lucky you're so tall," Selina commented.

"Lucky for us all," Annette said. "The combination of Payton's quick footwork and height means the other teams in the district won't stand a chance."

Payton listened to Annette half-heartedly. Her head was swimming. How was she expected to perform well in a sport she was just learning the rules for? She thought about calling her dad and pleading for him come back home to help her train.

"The last thing I'll tell you, for now, is that you cannot block or hit a serve you are receiving. Keep your arms down and wait for the ball to be passed at least once before you hit it over the net. But once a rally has started, meaning the ball is making its way back and forth between both sides of the court, then you can block and spike it all you want."

Coach Mike joined them. "How's our trio of newbies? Has Annette fried your brains yet?"

The girls laughed nervously. It was the first time he had talked to them directly. Payton still wasn't sure what to make of him. When they signed in as a team, he'd been relaxed and goofed around with the players, spitting out imitations of his favorite Hollywood stars. But as soon as the court had been cleared for the teams to warm up he'd gone Coach Sergeant again.

"Listen," he said, launching into a speech. "I know it's a lot to take in, but that's what camp is for—to turn newbies into All Stars over the space of a few days. Welcome to boot camp, girls. I'd love to say go out there and have fun, but that's not why we're here. We're here to ensure both our JV and varsity teams are ready to compete before September. Because you're new to the sport doesn't mean I'll take it easy on you girls. In fact, just the opposite. You have to prove to me more than any other girl here that you have the drive to win. If you can't handle that, you might as well walk out that door." He pointed to the exit.

Selina looked encouraged, and Neeka had her determined face on. Payton felt a bit frightened. However, she tried to copy Neeka's steely expression, though secretly, she squeezed her friend's hand.

****

Payton felt as if her arms were going to fall off. The JV teams were in the smaller gym doing drills with the camp instructors while the varsity girls took over the main stage. They'd been paired off to practice a drill called peppering, where two players served, passed, and hit the ball back and forth to each other. Serve, pass, hit. Serve, pass, hit. The cycle repeated indefinitely. Payton was partnered with Lacey, to her relief, but Lacey's patience with her didn't stop her arms from turning into spaghetti after what felt like the millionth serve.

"You're doing great," Lacey cheered, though Payton knew it was a lie. Every time she tried to pass the ball, it got flung in unpredictable directions. She understood the point of passing wasn't to keep the ball off the floor; it was to make sure the ball reached its desired target— Lacey. So why couldn't she get it right?

Good thing I'm not shooting arrows, Payton thought. *Lacey would be safe. I'm not sure about the other girls, though.*

After nearly being bonked in the head by a misfired ball, Annette abandoned her own partner and came over to inspect. "Don't search for the ball with your arms. Position yourself underneath the ball, right at your midline, by shuffling toward it. Then pass, facing your target.

The force behind your pass should be in your legs, not your arms."

When Payton's passes continued to go wild, Lacey grabbed the ball and set it on the ground. "Let me see your platform," she requested patiently.

Payton showed her.

"Well, here's part of the problem," she said, sounding almost thankful there was a cause to Payton's troubles. "Your arms aren't straight. You're keeping one arm higher than the other. It doesn't matter how well you aim; if your platform is off, the ball will be too."

Payton tried to keep her arms straight upon passing the ball, but something that was meant to be so simple was proving to be a challenge. Where being lanky and awkward was an asset in basketball, it wasn't winning her any brownie points in volleyball. *No wonder I never took up volleyball sooner*, she thought. *The few times I played volleyball in PE class, something must have put me off. Now I know what it was. I keep stumbling around.*

"Don't worry, you'll get it," Lacey said reassuringly.

They moved on to setting, but Payton didn't fare any better. Whenever Lacey passed her the ball, her big gangly hands kept pushing the ball low and forward instead of high in the air. It was humiliating. If she was experiencing this much trouble, she could only imagine how much trouble poor Neeka was having.

The day progressed slowly, a never-ending cycle of mishap after mishap. Lacey was encouraging, telling Payton it was only her first day and not to be too hard on herself, but she saw the aggravation in Annette's glances her way. She nearly dropped to her knees in thanks when a short break was finally allowed.

Instead of heading to the water cooler, Payton instead snuck over to the smaller gym to lend her friend some support, afraid she may have gotten Neeka in over her head. Volleyball was *way* more difficult than basketball. But what she saw was the exact opposite. Neeka was passing the ball with the same grace as some of the girls on the varsity team.

"Way to go, Neeka!" she shouted enthusiastically, though she was surprised Neeka was doing so well.

It was clear Payton would have to work a bit harder to catch up to the progress Neeka and Selina were making. She felt funny. Never before had there been a sport she wasn't automatically good at. Watching Neeka shuffle around the court with a newfound confidence about her planted a new doubt within Payton.

What if I am never good enough?

****

"We have a scrimmage tonight," Annette informed Payton, just as the clock hit 4:00 pm.

Camp was supposed to be over for the day. Payton looked toward Neeka, dismayed. They had plans to have a sleepover and play the new Talking Wizard game Payton's dad had sent her from Cincinnati. All she wanted to do was go home, eat dinner, chat with Neeka, and put the humiliating day at camp behind her.

"I thought we were done for the day," Neeka said. "Look, everyone is leaving."

"This is camp," Annette retorted. "You play basketball in your sleep."

"Don't be so harsh," Lacey scolded, joining them. "Remember, they're only fourteen." She turned to the girls. "Coach Mike arranged it. Varsity is playing, not JV, but the JV team is still expected to stay and watch. You're our biggest fans tonight," she said, affectionately pulling at one of Neeka's springy curls. "It's a closed scrimmage. No parents."

"I'm game," Payton said, trying to fake the confidence she did not feel.

"You'd better be," Annette said.

After they left, Neeka turned to her and grumbled, "She forgets, she's the one who called you. But I love Lacey."

"That sounds like a TV show my grandpa used to watch," Payton said.

Neeka moaned at the joke, but she took her arm and led her toward the gym to wait for the scrimmage to begin. Payton felt comforted by Neeka's presence. Given her bad performance today, Payton was starting to look up to her. Neeka had never been the best at basketball, yet she never gave up. She always pushed herself to keep going. Payton realized she could learn a lot from her friend.

Forty-five minutes later—after everyone on the Hickory Academy volleyball team had successfully reached their parents to inform them of the delay—Payton found herself standing in the near-empty gymnasium holding the ball in the air with her left hand, ready to serve it over the net with her right. They were already well into play against the Hawks, but this was her first serve of the match. Scratch that. Of her entire volleyball career. She felt off-center and double-checked to make sure she was still standing behind the end line. One foot over and it'd result in a side-out. She didn't want the point to go to the other team because of a stupid error.

Taking a deep breath, she dropped the ball slightly before punching it with her fist, but her serve wasn't powerful enough, and it hit the antenna attached to the side of the net, which qualified as a side-out. The point went to the other team. It was their turn to serve. Instead of feeling embarrassed, she only felt relief. At least now the pressure was off, if only temporarily.

Funny, in all the other sports she played, she thrived off pressure, drank it up. She had an ability to ignore everything around her, from screaming fans to the glaring scoreboard, and just let herself free, allowing her body to take charge while all unnecessary thoughts and emotions disappeared.

But not today.

One day in and volleyball camp was already proving to be a nightmare. She was so frustrated. She thought camp would be a lot of fun, but it was being significantly pushed down the list of exciting new activities she'd tried this summer.

"Payton, it's yours," one of the varsity girls shouted as a high serve came flying her way. She tried to even out her arms and pass it to Lacey, the setter, but the ball somehow landed in the basketball hoop tucked away in the back corner of the gym near where she was standing.

"Wrong sport," Lacey yelled, laughing.

"Wait, what camp am I at?" Payton joked back.

The next rally lasted a bit longer. The ball flew back and forth numerous times before Hickory Academy successfully tipped it over the net. Along the way, Payton had made a few successful passes, refusing to repeat her basketball hoop shame.

Blocking came easiest. Being the tallest girl on the court meant she could easily prevent the ball from hitting empty space on their side. The key was to figure out which hitter planned to spike the ball over. She needed to work on it, but she knew it was only a matter of learning to read the other team's body language.

As soon as Payton rejoined the back line after a rotation, Annette suddenly appeared at her side, wearing a white T-shirt instead of the blue one everyone else wore. Payton nodded and moved off the court to the sidelines. Annette was the team's *libero*, meaning she could replace any member of the back row whenever she wanted. It was a defensive mechanism to ensure there was stable passing in the back.

"Stay warm, you'll be back in later," Coach Mike instructed. "You're improving, Moore. Your footwork is excellent, some of the best I've seen. It's the rest of you that's moving a bit too slowly. But I suspect you'll eventually do, as long as you practice like there's no tomorrow."

"I will," Payton promised.

Because it was a scrimmage and the girls had spent a long day at camp, the teams were only playing the best out of three sets instead of the usual best out of five. By the third set, Payton was exhausted and more discouraged than before. No matter how she positioned herself before striking, the ball kept going into the net. They had recruited her onto the team to strike. What good was she if she couldn't score?

When the final set ended, with the win going to the Hawks, Payton longed for the comfort of her pajamas. There would be no Talking Wizard game tonight. She just wanted to go to bed. Though frustrated by her performance that day, she carried Coach Mike's semi-compliment with her to sleep. *"Yours is some of the best footwork I've seen."* It gave her hope in an otherwise miserable day.

****

By the last day of camp, Payton could see progress in her game. Her serves were still falling a little short, but her spikes were actually making it over the net, though they lacked the force of the other varsity members, or the *Bam Boom* as Lacey called it. She was thankful she was improving, but she knew she could do better. At least the week ended with Hickory Academy winning their final scrimmage.

During the car ride home after the scrimmage, neither Payton nor her mom had much to say to each other, both living in different worlds. For once, Payton didn't mind. Though her dad understood her way better than her mom did, she wouldn't have been able to face disappointing him with how uncoordinated she had been at volleyball camp. She was glad she didn't have to talk about it.

"Put a Band-Aid over your wounds and carry on," Neeka had said to her before they parted ways, but her friend's words had been of no comfort.

She'd miss Neeka, who was now on her way to her grandma's house in Georgia for a short stay, but high school would be starting soon. At least preparing for such an exciting step would help take her mind off volleyball for a while. As houses blurred past them in the car, Payton started planning what she'd bring her first day of school. Being a private school, the students of Hickory Academy had to wear a uniform, but they were able to pick their own backpacks, school supplies, and jackets.

Without warning, her mom pulled into the parking lot of a computer store.

"Will you be long?" Payton groaned, already reaching for the stereo. She usually listened to music in the car while her mom did her shopping.

"You're coming with me," her mom said, a twinkle in her eye. "I may not know much about volleyball, but I know my own daughter. I know you're worrying, Payton. I also know you'll refuse to talk about it, but I still want to be there for you. I was saving this for later in the week, but now is as good a time as any. You're about to enter high school, my sweet little girl..." Her mom choked up.

"Mom," Payton admonished, embarrassed.

Allison cleared her throat and continued. "I thought it was time you had your own laptop."

"Are you serious?" Payton screeched, racing out of the car.

Ms. Moore wrapped her arm around her daughter's shoulders. "Follow me, Miss High School. Your new computer awaits."

As they walked toward the entrance of the computer store, all thoughts of volleyball disappeared from Payton's mind, the week of camp horror nothing more than a fading memory.

CHAPTER 4

"Biology 101," Payton stated, reading her schedule as she and Neeka entered their first class of high school. She was glad they'd landed a few classes together, especially Biology, since it was the first period of the day and required a lab partner. If she had to dissect toads, she wanted it to be with Neeka.

This was it! They were officially high school students! Payton couldn't believe it. Her hands were sweaty, but more from excitement than nerves.

Jamari had dropped the girls off before heading to his own school, showering them with "advice" on how to survive. Her favorite comments during the car ride to Hickory Academy that morning were "Don't eat the gum off the back of the seats" and "If you have to choose between homework or toilet paper, choose toilet paper." He was such a nut.

Though she'd been there before on visits, walking through Hickory Academy High School, knowing she was now a student, made everything about the school seem bigger and more important. The corridors were wider. The lockers were taller. Finally, she wouldn't have to bend down to her knees to open the combination lock. She felt different, like she was part of a secret club only people her age knew about.

"More like Boyology 101," Neeka observed as they found a lab table and sat down, admiring the faces around them. There were only three other girls in their Biology class. The rest of the seats were filled with slugs and snails and puppy-dog tails.

"How did this happen?" Payton giggled.

Neeka shrugged her shoulders. "I don't know, survival of the ugliest?"

Payton pulled out her navy Titans notebook and matching pencil case and set them proudly on the table. "I still can't believe we're finally in high school."

"We're freshmen!" Neeka exclaimed.

The girls clasped their hands together and squealed.

"My goodness, how can two young females create such a terrible noise," a man said softly, more to himself than anyone else, as he entered the room.

Payton and Neeka immediately fell silent.

Dr. B, their Biology teacher, was infamous at Hickory Academy. Most kids and parents thought him to be a stuffy ole English professor, even though he was only in his thirties. The story was he used to lecture at the university but grew bored and wanted to teach high school students instead. Payton mused over this. He was young for an adult, younger than her parents, but he wore reading glasses, which he had clipped to his collar, and he had grey streaks running through his dark hair. The entire effect made him seem older than he was, especially since his posture was slightly slouched, just like the old university professors they always showcased in the movies.

"It appears I left my attendance sheet in the teachers' lounge," Dr. B declared, searching across his table at the front of the classroom. "I'll be right back."

So this is high school. Teachers aren't afraid to leave their classrooms unattended, Payton thought as soon as he left.

"What does Dr. B stand for?" she asked Neeka.

"Dr. Boring," one of the boys at the table next to them answered.

"Dr. Bad Breath," another said.

"Dr. British," a girl chimed in.

"Isn't it obvious?" said a boy across the room. "It stands for Dr. Biology."

As it turned out, Dr. B stood for Dr. Ronald Beamon. He lived up to his no-nonsense reputation. As he read out the syllabus, it was obvious he was going to be tough, treating them like mini college students rather than high school freshman. But with the extra responsibility, he was also giving them special freedoms. Instead of raising their hands and asking to use the bathroom, they were free to take the pass on the wall whenever they chose, as long as it wasn't during a quiz or test. They were also allowed to choose their own lab partners. The privileges he gave them were little, but Payton thought they were cool.

To start the semester, he made them watch a video on genetics. Afterwards, he went to the whiteboard and began discussing the difference between genotypes and phenotypes. "Not all genes are observable. You may have blue eyes, but you can still carry genes for brown eyes. A genotype is all the genes an organism carries in their DNA. A phenotype is just the ones that have manifested to shape how the organism looks and functions. Take this down in your notes. You'll need to know it for upcoming experiments we'll be conducting on genetics."

Payton scribbled into her Titans notebook. It was all a little bit too much for her brain to take in. She'd only been in high school for less than an hour!

"I know he makes you want to yawn when he talks, but I think he's kind of cute," she whispered to Neeka as Dr. B drew something called a chi square. "Kind of like a grown up Harry Potter."

"You have been playing too much of that Talking Wizard game," Neeka hissed back.

Dr. B turned around from the whiteboard. The girls instantly pretended to be studying their notes. When he resumed writing, Neeka leaned in closer to Payton.

"It's going to be so weird splitting up for volleyball practice today," she admitted. "I've never played a team sport without you there."

"It's only for practice. Technically, I'm on both the JV and varsity teams, so I'll still be with you on the court during matches, just like at camp." She tried to sound reassuring, but she knew exactly what Neeka was feeling. Payton had played tennis and soccer without Neeka, but this was different. This was something they had started together. Splitting up for practice felt like flying a kite with no string.

"I have to admit, I'm really enjoying volleyball, way more than I thought I would. I just wish you were there. We do everything together," Neeka insisted.

"I know," Payton said. "In many ways, I wish I'd only joined the JV—"

She didn't have time to finish her sentence. Dr. B turned around again. This time, he looked directly at them. Removing his glasses from the tip of his nose, he scowled, not at all impressed.

The girls looked down, embarrassed, but as soon as his back was turned, they broke out into silent giggles.

****

"Volleyball season is short. Over the next two months, there's no time to make mistakes. If you want to win the District Championships, you better start winning now," Coach Mike said, hollering at the team. "I don't want any excuses. If you're performing badly, you better figure out why and fix it quick if you want to stay on this team. This ain't no rodeo, folks—this is war."

Payton looked around. She wondered if his threat was genuine. The numbers only just barely made up an entire team as it was. They had eight girls in total, six starters and two subs. A team usually had at least nine players. However, the way Coach Mike roared, she almost believed in his threat.

She wondered how Neeka's practice with Coach Gina was going. The JV team was practicing at the middle school gym. The walk there only took a few minutes, but she felt as if her friend was miles away. Maybe it was a good thing they were separated. At least then, with no one to compare her to, Coach Mike might not realize how badly Payton was doing for a newbie.

"Annette, during drills today team up with Payton, aka I-Like-To-

Serve-It-Into-The-Net. Make sure the only thing the ball touches is the dust on the other side of the court."

Never mind, he knows.

To warm up, the team jogged around the gym for five minutes, then stretched. After the excitement and stress of her first day in high school, Payton found it refreshing to loosen her muscles. She tried to enjoy her temporary bliss while it lasted, pushing from her mind what was soon to come.

"How was your first day?" Annette asked, reaching for her toes.

She can be nice when she wants to be, Payton thought. *Or when she wants something. Something I'm not sure I can give her—victory.*

"It went really well. Only I'm stuck with Dr. B for Biology."

Annette rolled her eyes. "He's the worst. I used to call him Dr. Big Bird because he stretches his neck out when he's teaching."

"That's a good one," Payton said, making a mental note to tell it to Neeka.

"I remember one day, I was really upset because my cat had just died. I tried to hide it, but Dr. Big Bird caught me crying. After class, when all the other kids had left, he made a huge deal about it. Insisted on calling a parent-teacher conference. When I told him why I was upset, he didn't believe me. My mom had to show him a photo of poor Paw Paw's freshly dug grave to prove to him there wasn't anything else going on with me. What a creep."

"Yikes," Payton uttered, not sure how to process this new information about Dr. B.

After several warm ups to practice their lateral moves across the court, one of which involved jumping in and out of plastic squares laid across the ground, the team moved on to developing their passes. Divided in half, the team stood on opposite sides of the net facing each other in staggered lines. Annette stood at one end with a hammock-style cart full of balls. One by one, she passed the balls down the line. Each girl had to pass the incoming ball over the net to a teammate on the opposite side.

Just like at camp, Payton kept messing up, but she wasn't the only one. Ball after ball hit the floor. "Come on, focus," Annette yelled at the team. Remembering Coach Mike's instructions, she singled Payton out. "Bend your knees. Straighten your arms."

Payton tried, but she grew frantic and her body rebelled, doing the exact opposite. She straightened her legs and bent her arms. She looked like an accordion, twisting and turning around.

Stupid volleyball, she thought.

Finally, Coach Mike blew his whistle. "What was that?" he asked them all. "That was some of the worst volleyball I'd ever seen. The first graders at the elementary school could win against you in a scrimmage. Who's actually been practicing at home?"

Everyone raised their hand except Payton. She immediately shot her hand up too, hoping Coach Mike didn't see her hesitation. She felt bad for lying, but she didn't want to be the center of any more attention that day.

"You all practiced? I am finding that incredibly hard to believe," he ranted. "I see I've been too soft with all of ya. No more Mr. Nice Coach. We're going to practice our serves next. If you miss a serve, you owe me ten pushups."

That doesn't sound so bad, Payton thought.

"On the other side of the court, directly in the line of fire of your fellow teammates as they serve," he finished.

Payton caught Lacey's eye. The older girl frowned. Payton knew what she was thinking.

She's only fourteen.

Lacey raised her hand to protest, but Payton shook her head, indicating for her not too. She was a star athlete. No matter their age, athletes were used to getting thumped with a ball.

Still, Payton wasn't going to volunteer to be pommelled by her teammates. She stood at the back as they lined up to serve, praying a fire alarm went off before her turn came up.

Please Neeka, pull the alarm, she thought hard, wondering if, because they spent so much time together, they shared the same psychic ability twins claimed to have.

Obviously not. Payton's turn came. Inevitably, between her nervous, shaking arms and inability to focus, the ball went straight into the net.

"Big surprise, Moore," Coach Mike yelled. He pointed to the other side of the court. "Dead girl walking."

Payton did her pushups quickly and managed to avoid being hit by the ball. But she netted her serve again, and wasn't so lucky the second time around. A ball caught her right on the back of her head.

"Careful," she heard Lacey scold whoever hit her.

As practice continued, and Payton managed to miss all her serves, it started to become more than obvious that she was now the game. The varsity girls enjoyed aiming for her as she did her pushups. Thankfully, many missed, but a few bonked her.

When it was time to move on to the weight room, Payton nearly collapsed with relief.

"Having fun?" Annette asked as she helped Payton set up the weights on the squat machine.

Payton didn't know how to answer.

"Toughen up, it was just a joke," Annette said. "I know Coach is being hard on us, but we have a tough season ahead. In a way, you kinda summarize our entire team. Just because we're only in our third season doesn't mean the other teams will go easy on us. They will destroy us every chance they get, especially Demonbreun High. They show no mercy; that's why they're the District Champions. This is my last year, Payton. I know you're only a freshman, so it's hard to understand, but I really want to leave here as champions ourselves. I helped to start the volleyball legacy at Hickory Academy. I was here when the volleyball team served its first rally, and I want to be here when we bring home our first trophy."

Payton was beginning to understand why Annette was so obsessed with winning. Payton could identify with her. She felt the same need for glory in basketball. The difference was, she didn't let it consume her. Not the way it did Annette. The senior had taken the drive to win to a whole new level. It was a shame. Payton always thought senior year should be about having fun. She vowed that when she became a senior, her main focus would be her friends, not her trophy case.

****

At home later that night, her father called. Payton leapt for her hot-dog phone. She'd been waiting impatiently for his call since dinner. She wanted to tell him all about her first day of high school. He'd been a student of Hickory Academy as well. When she graduated, her photo would hang alongside his in the grand hallway. She had so many questions to ask him. Like if Mrs. Turtle, the ancient librarian, had been there when he was a freshman.

"Hi, Daddy," Payton sang as she answered.

"Hi, baby girl. I really miss you."

"I miss you too."

"How was your volleyball practice today?"

Straight to sports, as usual.

Payton hesitated. Her father had raised her to be the best. How could she possibly explain to him she'd been terrible at volleyball so far? That her talents as an athlete were limited?

"Pretty good. I'm still trying to get a hang of things. Until today, my only real experience was at camp. I wanted to practice more in between camp and school, but Neeka was at her grandma's and you were away... but it's pretty good."

"You're a pro. Before you know it, they'll be making you captain. I'm so proud of you, honey."

"Thanks Daddy," Payton said quietly, swallowing the words, the taste of frustration in her mouth. "Want to hear about my first day of high school?"

"Yes, of course. Sorry. I've had a long day. That's why I'm only calling you now. Please, tell me all about it."

"I saw your picture in the grand hallway. Daddy, you never told me you had a mullet and a moustache."

"Those were the times, baby girl." He laughed at the memory. "I wish they'd take that silly thing down."

"When I have my graduation photos taken, I think I'll wear a fake moustache. Just so we can match."

"Payton, I'd give you million bucks to see that happen."

CHAPTER 5

"Ouch, that's my hair!"

"Neeka, that's my arm!"

Neeka giggled. "Sorry, I thought it was my leg."

The small downstairs bathroom of Hickory Academy High School had been transformed into a flustered mess of legs and arms as the JV team scrambled into their uniforms. Their protests as they stepped on each other echoed across the old piping and linoleum floor. The bathroom was part of the original wing of the school, before the extension had been added.

Neeka pulled her blue and white jersey over her head, thankful for her short hair, then checked her cellphone for what felt like the hundredth time that day.

Still no reply.

"Tell me again why we didn't go to the locker room to change," Selina asked crossly, squished against the back near the window.

"We don't have time. We only have a few minutes before class starts," Payton mumbled as she pulled her socks up, consequentially bumping her behind against one of the other girls, who went sprawling into a bathroom stall.

The bathroom erupted into laughter.

"Oh, really funny, guys," the girl said, though she was laughing too.

"We only have three minutes to get to class!" Neeka announced.

"Hurry it up, ladies!"

"My class is all the way upstairs!" Selina yelped and began pushing her way through the crowd, but got stuck between an arm tying her shoe and another pulling her hair into a ponytail.

"Let's go!" Neeka yelled, taking charge. "None of us can risk detention for being late."

The girls listened to her. They began pouring out of the bathroom, slowly at first as they scrambled past each other. One girl went running down the near empty corridor missing one shoe, which she held in her hand.

Their first match of the season was that afternoon. They needed to leave as soon as the final bell rang, because the match was on the other side of Nashville, so they'd decided to change in the downstairs bathroom before their last class of the day. It was that or try to change in an even tinier van. At least the bathroom had mirrors. And room to stand, if only barely.

Neeka looked at her cellphone again, the last to leave.

Please, please, please, she thought.

Payton was just ahead of her, but she stopped and turned around. "Everything okay, jelly bean?"

"My mom is supposed to text me to let me know if dad can come to the match or not."

Payton looked sympathetic. She put her arm around Neeka's shoulders. "Don't worry, if he can't make this match, he'll make others."

Neeka appreciated Payton's support. She knew her friend was experiencing a similar situation with Brandon (do you mean her dad?) so she could fully understand how she felt.

"It's just, I'm finally doing okay at a sport. I want him to see me play. I want him to be proud."

An uneasy look passed across Payton's face, but Neeka couldn't read it.

Together, they headed to their last classes of the day, each making it into her seat right as the tardy bell rang.

On the van ride to their match against the Vikings, amid the noise of the other JV girls gossiping loudly about their fellow high school students, Neeka finally got the news she'd been waiting for.

I'm sorry, honey. Dad is caught up with work tonight. Jamari and I will cheer extra loud. X Mom

Her shoulders slumped forward. She really wanted her dad here. It was her first match of volleyball ever, at a competitive level at least. He'd never seen her in a volleyball jersey before. She didn't understand why he couldn't find someone to cover his shift, if even for a few hours. It just didn't make sense to her. Wasn't she more important than some lousy hospital?

Tears began to swell around the corner of her eyes, but she wouldn't let them fall. She was tougher than that. She sniffed them away.

But she couldn't hide how upset she was from Payton, who was sitting next to her in the van, knee to knee. Having obviously read the text over Neeka's shoulder, Payton hugged her but said nothing, allowing her time to regain her composure.

The rest of the van ride was a bit tense. Neeka knew Payton wanted to say something but didn't know what. Finally, just as the van pulled into the parking lot of the Vikings, Payton said, "Hey, Neeka, how did Vikings communicate in the past?"

"Do I want to know?" Neeka asked with dread in her voice.

"Through Norse code."

"Payton, that is absolutely the worst joke you've ever told." Neeka rolled her eyes but appreciated her friend's efforts. She even began to smile.

"What about this one—why did the bike need a stand to stay upright?"

Returning to her good humor, Neeka put a hand up. "Please, do us all a favor and never, ever tell us the punch line to that joke."

"Because it was two-tired."

"Stop, please, stop," Neeka chuckled, jumping out of the van. She was feeling better. The excitement of the first match was starting to set in. She hadn't experienced this kind of anticipation before. It was a new experience—being in the starting lineup and knowing you weren't a complete goof on the court.

The Vikings gymnasium was nearly full. Volleyball wasn't a huge sport at Hickory Academy yet, so their numbers were small, but having nearly beat Demonbreun High at the District Championships the previous year, the Vikings volleyball teams, JV and varsity alike, attracted huge numbers. The bleachers were toppling with fans wearing huge metal helmets with horns sticking out on either side. Many had double Vs painted across their faces. It was pandemonium.

During the coin toss to decide who would serve first, the Vikings fans started shouting, "Strike them down, strike them down!" led on by the cheerleaders.

"I can't believe they have cheerleaders at their volleyball matches," Selina exclaimed as one of the Vikings male cheerleaders threw a girl up high into the air. "I wonder when the Hickory Academy cheerleaders will start coming to our matches."

"When we bring home a trophy," Payton answered.

The fans roared when the Vikings won the coin toss. They chose to serve first. A lot of teams did, thinking it might give them an advantage in the final set, especially when they had a star server like the Vikings did. Brianna Jones was known for her aces—serves that were nearly untouchable, diving hard and fast to unprotected floor on the opposing team's side.

Thankfully, Brianna Jones was on the varsity team. Neeka wouldn't have to worry about her today. She'd studied the girl during camp, noticing how Brianna always took her time on the serve, never letting the noise around her become a distraction. It was then that Neeka had first realized that volleyball wasn't just about strength. It was also about intelligence.

After the players, coaches, and officials had been introduced, the national anthem played, and all players had shaken each other's hands, the referee blew her whistle, indicating the starting lineup of both teams to take their places on the court and for the coaches and remaining players to have a seat on the bench.

Neeka waited with her knees bent, ready to set as soon as they received the first serve of the match. They were going to play the best of out five sets. They would play to twenty-five points for the first four sets and fifteen points for the final set, but the score could go over because a team had to win a set by at least two points. Daunted by the volume of the Vikings fans, Neeka prayed Hickory Academy wasn't crushed by their opponents.

She quickly looked up into the bleachers for her mom, hoping for some encouragement. Mrs. Leigh blew a kiss down to her daughter. Jamari mouthed, "Don't trip."

The referee blew her whistle again from the top of what looked like an extra tall stepladder and signaled for the Vikings to begin service. Seconds later, the ball soared over the net. A girl in the back row yelled, "Got it!" and passed it on to Neeka. As if in slow motion, she watched as the ball sailed into the air high above her. She positioned herself directly underneath it, listening as Selina yelled "Me!" Facing Selina, Neeka formed a triangle over her forehead and, once she felt the smooth surface of the ball land on her fingers, extended her arms out, pushing the ball back into the air toward Selina, who was already forming a bow and arrow shape with her arms, ready to pound the ball over the net.

She'd set the ball a little low, but Selina managed to strike it over. A girl in the back row of the Vikings' side reached it just before it hit the floor and passed it on to her setter. The strike back over to their side of the net went straight toward Payton. Standing in an awkward ready position, Payton barely had enough time to pass it. The ball flew straight toward Neeka, twisting in the air. She knew she couldn't get a good set with it, so instead, she decided to use the velocity of the ball toward her advantage. She extended her fingers and tipped it over the net.

"Dink!" one of the Vikings shouted, but it was too late. They'd planned on blocking the ball from a hitter, not the setter. The ball landed on the floor, earning Hickory Academy the first point of the match.

The girls quickly hugged in celebration then prepared to serve. They played well, engaging in a few rallies with the Viking girls that left the fans at the edge of their seats. "Hot dog!" she heard one of the fans yell. "Someone better make the kill soon or we ain't never getting out of here."

A few rotations into the set, with the score close, it was finally

Neeka's turn to serve. She took her time, scanning the court in front of her, enjoying the time she was allowed to apply some intellect to her movements. The back row of the Vikings moved forward toward the ten-foot line. It was obvious they expected the serve to go low, like some of her sets had been.

Think again, Neeka thought.

She served, and the ball landed in the unprotected back corner of the court.

"Nice one!" Selina yelled.

Neeka served again. This one dived toward the floor just after it crossed the net. Another point.

It became clear to the Vikings girls on the other side that they couldn't predict where Neeka's serve would land. And that she was a force to be reckoned with. They stood tenser, more focused, waiting for her to serve.

Neeka was delighted. Now she knew how Payton felt all these years. It was exhilarating being a good athlete. Volleyball was definitely her thing.

Coach Gina yelled her praise, jumping up and down like a cheerleader on the sidelines. Her designer sunglasses nearly toppled off the side of her head. "Good work, girls!" she shrieked. "Keep it up, Neeka."

The match continued, and before long, they were on their third set. As the ball was launched toward their side of the net, Neeka prepared to set. She signaled Payton, knowing her friend had the best opportunity to score a point, but Payton spiked it into the net. It wasn't the first time she'd done so that afternoon, but Neeka didn't reproach her for it. There was a learning curve when taking on a new sport. They all made mistakes.

The next time Neeka set for Payton, instead of spiking the ball over, she dinked it, tipping it off her fingertips to the other side. It earned a point because the Vikings weren't expecting it, but when Payton continued to dink it over, they were prepared and blocked it each time. Neeka knew Payton was losing her nerve. She wasn't dinking it out of strategy. She was giving up, reversing to a move she knew would make it over the net, even if it was ineffective. From that point forward,

Neeka mostly served to Selina or one of the better hitters on the team.

Neeka wanted to feel sorry for Payton, but she refused to, knowing she would have hated it if Payton had felt any pity for her all these years in basketball. She could read the frustration all over Payton's face, but Neeka didn't worry. Payton was a natural athlete. Once she finally orientated herself, she'd be unstoppable. She just needed a little practice.

Hickory Academy won the final set 11-15.

"Well done, girls," Coach Gina said, waving her arms enthusiastically as they came off the court after shaking the Vikings girls' hands. "I'm so proud of all of you."

Neeka accepted several pats on the back from her teammates before rushing up to the bleachers to where her family sat. As she climbed the steps, she removed the clip from the top of her head that kept her short, curly spirals out of her eyes while competing. Now that the match was over, she preferred them to hang loose.

Her mom hugged her as soon as she reached them. "Great job, baby," she said, beaming. She held up her smart phone. On the screen was a photo of the entire nursing staff at the hospital holding up a sign that said, "Go Neeka!" In the center of the photo, holding the sign, was her dad, a huge silly smile upon his face.

Neeka kissed the screen on the phone. "Love you, Dad. Wish you were here."

"Soon," her mom promised.

Jamari dramatically opened his mouth and stuttered, pointing to the court below. "You... you..."

"Stop," Neeka giggled.

Jamari stopped his act. "You were amazing, little sis! The best on the court by far. Who knew—you're an athlete after all!"

****

After a short recovery period, the JV team crowded together at the end of the varsity bench. The streets of Nashville were still baking under a scorching sun. Though the gym was air conditioned, the heat had managed to find its way in. Sweating, the JV girls kept their warm ups off, allowing the breeze from the open doors to cool them down. Exhausted from their first match, some sat on the floor, their backs propped against the legs of their teammates.

"We need some of those *monsieur* people," one of the girls decided.

Selina snickered. "*Monsieur* is the French way of saying Mister. I think you mean a *masseur.*"

"Excuse me for not passing French," the girl said sarcastically as she relaxed onto the gym floor. "Anyway, who cares what they're called. As long as they give a good massage, that's all that matters."

Neeka glanced back into the bleachers. Payton's mom was now seated next to Jamari, having made it down for the varsity match. She was glad. Payton needed all the support she could get. Her friend currently sat on the bench next to her, her head down. She wasn't starting, a fact that added salt to her ever growing wounds.

"Payton, this is your very first varsity match of the season. Who cares if you're on the bench—you're here! Anyway, it's only because you just played a JV match that you have to sit out for a little while," Neeka said, trying to comfort her. "Coach Mike would hardly put you in the starting lineup when you've just been hustling around for the last hour. He's doing it for your sake. You're tired."

When Payton refused to look up, Neeka continued. "You are an amazing blocker. A good number of those points were due to your blocking skills."

That caught Payton's attention. "Only because I'm tall," she replied, defeated. "It has nothing to do with ability."

"Come on, Payton," Neeka urged, trying to improve Payton's confidence. "Okay, so volleyball isn't coming easy to you. So what. Just practice more and stay determined. You'll be fine in no time."

When Payton refused to respond, they sat in silence until the referee signaled the start of play.

Neeka nudged Payton playfully. "The match is starting. Watch how Brianna Jones serves. She's a legend, but we can take her."

Payton looked up but immediately dropped her head down again.

Neeka wondered if it was time for Payton receive a dose of tough love. She needed to pay attention to the match in front of her instead of moping in her own self-pity. Payton was used to being good naturally. She could still be a fireball in volleyball, but this time, she would have to work hard for her fame. It was time Payton started pushing herself. That began with watching the match and studying her opponents.

In the fourth set, Payton was finally called to sub in.

"Destroy them," Neeka cheered excitedly. "Don't hold back!"

Predictably, Payton struggled, sending her strikes straight into the net, before giving up and returning to dinking the ball over. It was like watching the JV performance all over again. Neeka felt uncomfortable watching her friend. She'd never seen Payton play badly before, at anything, but her discomfort was more the result of mixed emotions. She didn't understand what was holding Payton back.

Then an unusual thing happened. As expected, Payton dinked the ball over. The other team anticipated this and were able to send the ball flying back over the net. A heated rally ensued, but instead of bracing for the battle, Payton dropped her head and began giggling uncontrollably to herself, as if she'd just told herself a joke.

Seriously, Payton's messing around at a time like this, Neeka fumed inwardly.

It was suddenly very clear to her exactly what her friend's problem was. She wasn't taking the game at all seriously. It infuriated Neeka. The other varsity girls were depending on Payton to do her best. They were a team, and all Payton could do was think of herself. Neeka knew Payton could do better if she would only apply herself more, but now, even though it was only their first match, she doubted if Payton really did deserve a spot on the varsity team.

CHAPTER 6

This is disgusting, Payton thought.

"Genes are hereditary. They're passed down from parents to their offspring. George, you get your black hair because of your parents. Payton, you get your green eyes because of your parents. Rose, you get your small nose because of your parents. And so on."

"Actually, Dr. B, George gets his black hair from a bottle. He wants to be the next Taylor Lautner. His hair is actually light brown," Rose informed the class. "I know because George is my cousin. All the men in our family have the same hair color."

None of this changes the fact that we have to touch flies!

"As I warned you yesterday, today we're going to study the hereditary traits of *Drosophila melanogaster*, also known as the common fruit fly. We'll be observing their phenotypes—the appearance of the flies. Physical traits are handed down to them through their genes, which they get from their parents, just like you and just like all organisms. Some phenotypes are genetic mutations, meaning there has been a change in the genes. A normal fruit fly has red eyes and long wings. This is known as a wild type. Please consult the charts I passed out earlier."

Payton looked down at the chart she was sharing with Neeka. It illustrated the different traits in fruit flies. Some had big eyes and others had little narrow ones. Some wings were long and oval, some thin and scraggly, and some curly. Her attention moved away from the chart to the actual flies fluttering around in a large vial on their lab table. It made Payton want to hurl. Give her a spider any day. At least they were predictable. What if a fly flew into her nose!

"Now, before I get too far into my lecture, we'll need to give the flies an anesthetic. This will keep them still long enough to observe them. Take the bottle in front of you, dip the brush into the liquid, then stick the brush into the vial of fruit flies and leave it there. Do it quickly to minimize the amount of flies that escape."

"Do you want me to do it?" Neeka asked.

Payton nodded her head.

It was the first thing they'd said to each other all morning. Payton had a varsity match that afternoon. JV were off the hook. Only varsity was playing, so it meant she might be allowed more playing time. She didn't want to repeat the same mistakes she'd been making during matches, but ever since playing the Vikings, her improvement had plateaued. Her skills weren't developing fast enough. Never before had she felt this sensation of panic before playing sports. The only way she could deal was to shut off for a little while. She hoped Neeka understood.

"Once they're asleep, we'll sort them into groups based on their hereditary traits…"

Dr. B carried on with the lecture, but Payton's mind didn't follow. Not only did varsity have a volleyball match that afternoon, but they also had their team dinner afterward. She was nervous. Now that she wasn't some shining golden girl on the court, her teammates hadn't been as friendly as they had at the start. They were all losing patience with her, especially Coach Mike. She was afraid they'd been using her this whole time. It was a common fear of hers—that people were only friends with her because of her athletic abilities and not because they had any real interest in her.

She suddenly realized Neeka was saying something to her.

"What?" Payton asked, distracted.

"Are you looking forward to the varsity dinner tonight? It's a great pizza joint you're going to. Do you remember when Jamari got the nuclear beef—the one with all the jalapenos? I think it's the first time

I've ever seen him cry real boy tears. He looked as if he was going to explode, his face was so red."

"Yeah." Payton didn't have much energy to respond with. She was too stressed out. Why couldn't she be better in volleyball? Maybe she could genetically mutate herself to be better.

It appeared the lecture was over and the class was moving on to preparing for the actual experiment. As they waited for the flies to fall asleep, they laid out paper towels and paint brushes, which they'd use to observe and sort the flies with. The day was going too fast for Payton. She willed the minutes to slow down, but they seemed to go faster. *You know the old saying, time flies when you're counting fruit flies.*

Halfway through the experiment, Dr. B came to their table. "What are your thoughts on the experiment so far?" he asked.

It's gross, was Payton's honest opinion, which she kept to herself. The truth was, she didn't have much to say. Letting Neeka do most of the work, she'd been lost in thought most of the experiment. She'd catch up later tonight by studying her notes, after the match and dinner were over. She learned better reading on her own than she did in class environments anyway.

"There are two different groups of fruit flies. The smaller fruit flies have darker pigmentation than the bigger ones," Neeka stated.

Dr. B looked pleased. "And why do you think this is so? Payton?"

Payton thought quickly. The only major cause she could think of for two different types of fruit flies was that one was male and one was female, just like how human male and females looked different from each other. "They two groups represent the different genders?" she guessed.

"Well done, girls. Gender can greatly influence phenotype. And which gender is the bigger fruit fly?"

"Boy," said Neeka.

"Girl," said Payton.

"Why do you say boy, Neeka?" he asked without revealing who was correct.

"Because boys tend to be bigger than girls in muscle mass."

"Payton?" He pointed to her.

"Because women have a harder time losing weight than men,

according to my mom. I figure that means evolution favors bigger women."

He approved of both their answers. "Those are very logical postulations. When it comes to the fruit fly, the females are actually the bigger gender. Bigger females can carry more eggs, so they have survived throughout the generations due to natural selection."

Whatever, I just want this experiment to end, Payton thought. *But not the school day*, she added quickly to whoever may be reading her thoughts. She'd be blowing her nose for the next week just to make sure there was nothing up there. Already, flies were starting to wake and escape into the room.

Her mind wondered back to volleyball. Neeka was talking again, but Payton could only nod, zoning in and out of the conversation. Finally, Neeka gave up and the two stopped talking completely. Neeka took charge putting the flies back into their vial.

At the end of class, Dr. B called for their attention. "You can go a few minutes early but come get your quizzes first."

Of course. The one day Payton wished school would go slowly, everything was going quicker than normal. Now first period was already over. That was one class closer to the varsity match that evening.

"I'll catch up with you," Payton said to Neeka, packing her backpack slowly, unwilling to let the day go by as fast as it was.

Neeka looked as if she were going to protest, but changed her mind and, giving her friend an encouraging smile, grabbed her quiz from Dr. B and left.

Payton was the last to pick up her quiz.

"Payton, I was wondering if you would mind staying behind a few minutes. I wanted to have a quick chat with you," Dr. B asked impassively as he handed her back her quiz. There was a bright red A circled across the top.

"Okay," Payton said timidly, unsure of what she had done wrong. As the quiz showed, her grades were okay. In fact, the last few days, she'd probably paid more attention in class than she had ever before. Well, that wasn't completely true. Her chats with Neeka had stopped. That was correct. But the fact that they no longer whispered through his lectures had more to do with the fact that her mind was on other things, mainly volleyball. That didn't necessarily mean she was paying attention, but she did go home at night and study her notes.

"Sit here," Dr. B instructed, indicating the seat next to his desk.

She sat tensely, waiting as he put away the last of the fruit fly vials. His desk was completely in order. She thought absentminded professor types were meant to be messy, but nothing was out of place. Even the stapler was pushed to the back corner, perfectly aligned with the edge. Actually, now that she thought about it, a clean desk did fit his more soft-spoken nature.

He sat down and removed his reading glasses, tucking them into his collar. He folded his hands then said, "Tell me, Payton, what has been on your mind today? Why so quiet?"

Really? She was in trouble for being too *quiet* in class? Was this really happening?

"Let me clarify," he said in his upper class, well-mannered English accent. "For the first time all week, I haven't once had to ask you and Neeka to stop distracting each other. Is there anything you would like to talk about? I'm here to help."

"I'm fine," Payton said. She really wanted to tell him to butt out, that it was none of his beeswax, but she would never dare talk to a teacher that way.

"High school is a precarious time. Though a lot of pressure for someone so young, it can shape your future. The key is not to get off track. You're an excellent student, Payton. Your participation and quiz grades so far have been excellent. I would even venture to say you're one of the best in the class. But in high school, even the best of the best can fall off track. My intention as a teacher is to help students stay focused, before they fall too far."

Or you're just being nosy, Payton thought. Instead, she faked a smile. "You don't have to worry about me. I'm just focusing on the match tonight," she said, hoping a partial truth would be enough to set her free from this horrendous conversation. She assumed Dr. B was the type of teacher who could sniff out a lie.

Though her defenses were up, she had to admit, it felt good knowing she was doing well. She especially liked how he'd categorized her as "the best of the best." It'd been a long time since she'd heard that. It was a much-needed boost to her confidence.

"So nothing's bothering you?" Dr. B raised an eyebrow.

"Nope." Payton shook her head. "Nothing. I'm gold," she said, copying her dad's favorite expression. "I'm just still figuring out how to balance school and sports. I'm sorry. I won't let a match distract me again."

He suddenly seemed disinterested, shuffling his papers. "Grand. Don't be late for your next class."

Payton shoved her quiz into her bag as she walked out the door. Dr. B was so strange. She thought of the story Annette had told her. What did he care? Why was he so involved? Maybe he should concentrate on his own life and stop acting like a hundred-year-old grandpa instead of the youngish man he was.

She shook the conversation away. There were more important things to think about. In less than seven hours, she had a varsity match to play.

****

Payton stirred her chocolate milkshake idly, staring at the half eaten pizza slice in front of her. The pepperoni was starting to go cold and the cheese was hardening into a gooey glop. She closed her eyes, exhausted, but more emotionally than physically.

At the pizza joint that evening, the varsity girls gathered in celebration. They'd won their match against Winston High. They were undefeated so far, winning every match of the season including their first against the Vikings. It gave them something extra to raise their colas too. But Payton was in no mood for cheers and laughter. She hadn't contributed to their win. The exact opposite, actually. After sitting on the bench for most of the match, she'd finally been called in to sub, but what had been a short lead grew even smaller as she made mistake after mistake. She'd nearly cost them the match. Coach Mike had even kicked a chair before pulling her back off the court. But thankfully, they'd won.

She remembered looking up at Coach Mike after failing to pass a ball that had come to their side of the net hard. He'd dropped his head and folded his arms, clearly frustrated, angry even. For a split second, an image of her father replaced Coach Mike. She saw her dad pacing impatiently by the bleachers, regret written across his face.

Thank goodness her dad hadn't been there. He would have been so ashamed. There probably hadn't been a single moment when Coach Mike was pleased with her. Thinking back to the day Annette recruited her, she realized what an idiot she'd been to accept. She was never going to get any better.

She knew it, and so did her teammates. She was beginning to sense they no longer wanted her on the team. She didn't blame them, but it still hurt. Since the end of the match, no one even attempted to talk to her. They let her stew in her own gloom. Even Lacey avoided her gaze, but she suspected it had more to do with the fact the junior didn't know what to say. There were no words of comfort she could offer.

Payton Moore wasn't the type to let her teammates down. She usually led her team to victory. It was time to fix this. Things could not carry on this way. She needed to make amends by breaking down the wall forming between her and the rest of the volleyball girls. She might as well start tonight.

"Too bad Winston High isn't here. We could serve them a plate of nachos," she said loudly, catching their attention. The girls stopped talking to look at her.

"And why would we do that?" Annette asked snidely.

"Because then we could say, 'Sorry girls, but it's nacho day.'"

There was dead silence.

"That joke was worse than your serve," one of the girls jeered.

"And we all know how bad that is," another quipped, causing the rest of the table to erupt into laughter, everyone except Lacey, who sipped her water, hiding her disapproval of their mockery.

As soon as they were done snickering on her behalf, they returned to their conversations, blocking her out. It confirmed Payton's fears. They never had any interest in becoming her friend. They had used her, but because she wasn't as good at volleyball as they had hoped she would be, they were ready to cast her aside. She wished Neeka were there.

Neeka.

Something was happening between them, but she wasn't sure what or why. Payton knew she hadn't been completely herself because of the stress she was under, but it felt like that instead of helping her through it, Neeka was pulling away, becoming less interested in staying friends. They called each other less, and the conversations they did have seemed awkward and strained at times, especially at the mention of volleyball.

I'm just imagining it, Payton decided.

She was ready to go home, her appetite lost. It was only the start of high school, and already she was an outcast on the volleyball team, her coach refused to look at her, and a teacher had sat her down for a one-on-one meeting.

How am I going to survive? she pondered miserably.

CHAPTER 7

"That's it, girls! Communicate!" Coach Gina yelled. "Don't strike blind. You need to know where to hit. You also need to know where your other teammates are on the court. Talk to each other. You're all doing fab!"

"Sounds like she's about to break out the pom poms," Selina scowled, passing the ball to Neeka during practice. "Go team go."

Neeka giggled. She loved Selina's sense of humor. The two hadn't gotten along so well when the girls were in basketball, but now that she wasn't stuck to Payton's hip, she was able to get to know her teammate better. As it turned out, they were more similar than Neeka had originally thought. They both believed in hard work to get them where they wanted to go.

Coach Gina's optimism was wasted. Varsity was undefeated, but JV had lost its last two matches. But considering all the good players from the previous year had graduated to varsity this year, it meant the team was mostly made up of newbies and those still working on their skills. They weren't expected to be champions. That didn't stop Coach Gina, though. "We'll be number one!" she cheered.

"Something weird happened in the hall today," Neeka revealed, ignoring her coach as she confided in Selina. "Annette actually came up and talked to me. It was completely out of the blue. She usually just ignores me, but today she asked how I was enjoying high school so far.

She was so nice. It freaked me out."

"Wow," Selina said, preparing to strike the ball. "Maybe she wants you to do her homework."

"Or carry all their equipment to the next varsity match," Neeka speculated, sniggering.

"Seriously, be careful," Selina warned. "Annette is never nice unless she wants something. Your family isn't worth millions, is it? Maybe she wants to buy her way into the District Championships."

The middle school gym doors suddenly opened, and Coach Mike appeared. Coach Gina looked him over uncertainly. She obviously hadn't been expecting his visit.

"Coach, nice to have you here," she said, regaining her composure. She smoothed her hands over her expensive-looking sports leggings.

"Gina," Coach Mike greeted, then quietly made his way to the bleachers and sat down.

Selina shot Neeka a questioning look. Shrugging, she returned to their drill. She had no clue why Coach Mike would join them during the last fifteen minutes of practice. He usually left all the JV coaching up to Coach Gina.

Coach Gina blew her whistle. "All right, girls. That was fantastic. Line up at the end line. We're going to practice our serves." The girls did as they were told. "Up to now, we've focused on our underhand serves. But that was easy pick'ns. A bunny rabbit could serve an underhand serve. You girls have grown out of it, so now we're going to perfect our overhand serves. They're a bit harder to master, but more effective in gameplay."

Ball in hand, she stood at the end line, demonstrating as she spoke. "For the most basic overhand serve, stand with your feet apart. The foot in line with your non-dominating hand should be slightly forward. Take the ball into your non-dominating hand, toss it up about two feet, and pound it with the bottom palm of your dominating hand. For most of you, that will be your right hand." She served the ball. It made a loud smacking noise on impact with the floor, like thunder cracking. She may be loud and overly upbeat, but Coach Gina was good. There was no denying that. She'd won quite a few trophies during her college career. "Remember, as soon as you serve the ball, return to your defensive ready position."

She grabbed another ball from the cart. "We'll practice the basic overhand serve for now, but before we do, I want to show you a few other serves, so you know what you're prepping for. A float serve is like a basic serve, but you ensure your hand is flat and firm when you make contact, hitting the middle of the ball. This sends it low and forward, just skimming above the net." She didn't hit the ball, but she mimicked the movement, showing how her wrist stayed straight.

"Another serve is called a topspin serve. Essentially, you do everything the same, but you connect with the bottom half of the ball and you drop your wrist forward after making contact so that the ball spins and drops. A topspin serve moves higher than a float serve, making it difficult for the other team to receive because you can find deep corners or aim at weak passers."

She backed up further behind the end line. "Now, a jump serve can be a variation of both a float serve and a topspin serve. In a jump serve, you throw the ball into the air as you step, then take another couple of steps for momentum and jump into the air to make contact with the ball. So, a float jump serve would look like this…"

Coach Gina took two steps, threw the ball a few feet into the air, took a few more steps then jumped up to hit the ball. It flew low, gliding just over the net.

"And a topspin jump serve looks like this…"

Before moving, she threw the ball high into the air, about twenty feet. Then she took about four steps forward, jumped, and slammed the ball across the net. It traveled far, nearing the back of the court. The girls applauded.

Selina raised her hand. "Sometimes, you just hear the expression jump serve on its own. Does that mean a float jump serve or a topspin jump serve?"

Her usually perky self, Coach Gina answered. "Great question! It can be a little confusing, but if you hear the term jump serve on its own, it usually refers to a topspin jump serve. It's the hardest to do. Actually, there are no girls within our district this year that can do a topspin jump serve. That applies to both JV and varsity."

She blew her whistle after all questions were answered. "Okay, now it's your turn. But I don't want to see anyone going for a jump serve just yet. Coach's orders. Stick with getting a basic overhand serve over the net. Once you're able to do that, if you're feeling adventurous, you can try the float or topspin serves, but no jumping. You have to dominate the fundamentals before moving up."

Knowing Coach Mike was watching from the bleachers, the girls worked extra hard. By the time practice ended, they were in bits. Neeka didn't think she had ever sweated so much in such a short time.

"Shag the balls!" Coach Gina requested, indicating for the girls to collect the mass of balls that were lying around the court after their serving exercise. They returned the balls to the hammock-style cart.

As the girls threw towels around their necks and gulped water to cool off, the two coaches had a private conversation in the corner. Neeka studied them carefully. Coach Gina nodded, agreeing to whatever Coach Mike was saying, but she seemed reluctant, as if she agreed only because she had to. Then Coach Mike slipped out the door.

"Great work again, girls," the woman praised as she joined them. "You're all superstars. Neeka, let's have a chat," she said as the other girls headed toward the locker room.

She waited until every last girl had left the gym before she spoke. "You've exceeded all our expectations. I think you've found your calling, misses. You're a natural volleyball player. The next Misty May."

Neeka blushed at the compliment. Misty May was one of the most successful volleyball players of all time. "Thank you," she gushed.

"Anyway, Coach Mike is especially impressed. He'd like to see you in his office immediately."

"Right away," Neeka said. She headed out the opposite door, leading toward the path that connected the middle school to the high school. She would change later.

Neeka wasn't worried. She knew she wasn't in trouble. But she was intrigued. What could he possibly want to see her for? Her only connection to the varsity team was Payton. Maybe he wanted Neeka to help Payton practice more, knowing they were best friends.

I can't make Payton do something she doesn't want to do, Neeka thought, sure she'd figured out at least part of the reason why she was being summoned to Coach Mike's office.

She knocked awkwardly on his door. She'd never really spoken to him before, not privately anyway. He tended to ignore the JV team when they sat on the bench to watch the varsity matches, though he was known to joke around with the girls outside of volleyball. Selina had run into him once at the supermarket, and he'd been nothing but fun and games, making her parents laugh at some *Saturday Night Live* reference.

"Leigh," he greeted her as she opened the door. She was surprised to find him sitting casually with his feet on the desk eating out of a bag of popcorn that looked like it was left over from the movies. Cartoons were playing on a small portable TV next to him.

So this is what he looked like when they weren't competing. She wished she had a camera. The JV girls would trade a years' worth of their lunch money to see this.

"Yeah, Coach?" she asked, hanging out by the door.

"Listen, I don't want to take up your time, so I'll make this short and sweet. I want you to start practicing with the varsity team." He handed her a schedule, leaving fingerprints of butter on it from the popcorn. "From this point forward, you start practicing in the high school gym with me. Coach Gina isn't happy about it. She wanted to promote you to JV captain, but varsity is where the action is."

Her jaw nearly dropped. Did she hear correctly? Neeka never thought her name would be strung in the same sentence as varsity team. She couldn't believe he was considering putting her on the varsity roster.

"I'll be there, Coach," she confirmed before thanking him.

He turned the volume up on his cartoons. She took it as a sign to leave. *That was short and sweet.* Walking toward his office, she'd had the feeling he was going to compliment her, say something positive about the speed in which she was improving, but this was something else entirely. She had to keep herself from sprinting away with joy.

The locker room in the middle school gym was empty by the time she returned. Bursting to tell someone the good news, she was disappointed there was no one around. She immediately grabbed her cellphone. Instinctively, she input Payton's number, but hesitated. She wasn't sure this was the type of news Payton wanted to hear. Shaking her head, she searched her contacts then pressed the call button.

"Hi, Selina," Neeka squealed into the phone. "I must have just missed you. You'll never believe what happened…"

****

"Want to shoot some hoops?" Jamari asked as soon as the activity bus dropped Neeka off near their driveway. The sun was set low in the sky, but there was still plenty of light shining upon the hoop attached to their garage door for a quick game.

"You have an unfair advantage. You're a giant," she claimed. The truth was, he wasn't that tall. Not for a member of the boys basketball team. But he was massive compared to her short stature.

"You use that excuse every time. Come on, you've got to get your b-ball on before tryouts in October," he reminded her. "You used to come out here every night with me, but you haven't touched a basketball since volleyball camp. You are still trying out, aren't you?" It almost sounded like he was whining. Neeka never considered that, while she was occupied with volleyball, he was missing her.

"I'm afraid I might get confused and try to set the ball into the hoop," she said. She ignored his other question, unsure of what the future held, but she was pretty sure she'd still try out for basketball. It'd be hard to return, though, after the success she was experiencing with volleyball.

He made a clean shot, showing off his skills. "Hey, as long as it goes in, right? Member of the high school state basketball team— whhhaaatttt," he recited, breaking into his own personal cheer.

She set her backpack and equipment bag down and picked up the ball. She shot and missed. *Typical.*

"Practice makes perfect, as you always say," Jamari said. "Keep practicing and you might make a shot by the time you're ninety." He dunked the ball.

"Try me in a game of volleyball and we'll see who gets the last laugh," she challenged.

"Can't fault you there, sis. You've been a thunderstorm on the court, even if your team has lost their last two matches."

"Well, that may change soon."

"You gonna go back in time and change the scores?"

She laughed. "No. Coach has asked me to start practicing with the varsity girls." She sighed, wishful. "I really want to make varsity, Jamari. I have to."

Jamari looked cautious.

"What?" she demanded. She never knew her brother to hold back. "You jealous or something?"

"I'm happy for you, but did you consider who you might be replacing?"

Payton.

"It's not like that. Varsity doesn't have many subs. Coach Mike is probably just trying to fill in the roster. Payton and I will be sitting on the bench together. It'll be great. If I make the team, we'll both be playing JV and varsity."

Jamari relaxed. "Then go get 'em. If you keep playing like you have been, by the time you're a sophomore, you'll be on the starting lineup. Not bad for a girl who got a concussion in the sixth grade."

"What's so bad about that? Kids hurt themselves all the time."

"You were stretching your arm at the time, remember? You weren't even moving!" He burst out laughing, but asked her to follow him into the house.

She followed reluctantly, wishing he'd stop poking fun at her. Hadn't she finally proved herself as an athlete? The pea brain was probably just jealous because she was now going to be the star athlete of the family. The next Misty May, Coach Gina had said.

He marched her into the den where her parents kept all of his basketball trophies on a bookshelf. He cleared away the middle shelf, moving his trophies around. By the time he was done, only dust remained. She suddenly remembered it was on her chore list this month to dust. Her mom was very strict about their chores. She claimed it taught responsibility.

"Here you go," he said, flashing his hand toward the empty middle shelf.

"What's this?" she asked, puzzled.

"From this point forward, this is where all of your volleyball trophies will go. From what I've seen at your matches so far, I predict you'll be phenomenal, sis."

CHAPTER 8

Neeka watched with joint determination and pride as two class representatives hung a sign that read, "V is or Victory. Go Volleyball!" in the grand hallway. Varsity's undefeated record was igniting the interest of the student body at Hickory Academy. More than ever, Neeka was resolute in her goal to make it onto the varsity team.

Her stomach growled loudly, just as the quarterback of their football team walked by. He gave her a surprised look, as if asking, "Did that really just come from someone so tiny?"

My parents feed me, I swear, she wanted to yell, embarrassed, but instead scurried away to her locker where Payton waited for her, lunch bag in hand.

Payton's presence made her uneasy. She had not yet told her friend that she would be at the varsity practice that afternoon. She'd tried to a million times during Biology, but the words never came out. She was afraid Payton would be upset. At least Payton looked more cheerful than usual. Maybe her bad moods were easing. Now would probably be a good time to tell her.

"Yay! You're here!" Payton chanted as Neeka approached her. "I have the best news. As a surprise, my mom left a note in my lunch bag. Dad has scored tickets to the Tennessee Titans versus the Cincinnati Bengals game! He's driving down next Friday to pick me up and then we're heading to Cincinnati for the weekend. The best part—you're invited!"

"Isn't there a varsity match on next Saturday?" Neeka reminded her, reaching into her locker. Payton never would have missed a basketball game. She would have scheduled her visit to Cincinnati for the following weekend. Why should volleyball be any less important? Payton might not like it, but she was on the team. She had to step up or leave, not runaway to another state.

"So what, I miss one match. It's only a scrimmage, and this is a chance to spend time with my father. Coach will understand." Payton looked confused by Neeka's lack of excitement, probably thinking Neeka should be more sympathetic given she barely saw her father either.

"It's just—" Neeka began but was interrupted.

"Hi, girls," Lacey said, beaming. "I'm glad I found you two."

Please don't say anything, Neeka begged silently.

Her blonde ponytail bouncing, Lacey pulled out two homemade badges out of her bag. Shaped like volleyballs, they were made of white felt pasted onto cardboard with each of their names written across the middle in blue ink and sprinkled with green glitter.

"Since we're not allowed to wear our uniforms around school, at least not until last period," she teased, referring to the time the JV team had changed in the bathroom, "Annette thought it'd be a good idea if we all wore these on game days, to show the student body we're a team. We're also getting some team hoodies. They'll be delivered next week."

"That's so totally cool," Neeka said, immediately pinning her badge to her school uniform.

Payton accepted hers but said nothing.

"There's no match today," Lacey laughed. "But I like your enthusiasm, Neeka. I see why Coach asked you to start practicing with the varsity team. Don't take my spot," she kidded as she walked away.

Neeka winced and turned slowly toward Payton, who was stunned silent.

"So, yeah. I have some good news. Coach Mike was at our last JV practice an asked if I'd start training with you guys on varsity. Isn't that great! We'll be bench buddies."

Payton didn't seem so excited. "Wonderful," she said, but it came out sounding sarcastic. "Why didn't you tell me?" she asked, a flicker of irritation in her words.

"I didn't want to upset you... and I was obviously right," Neeka shot back, then softened her tone, not wanting to get into a fight. It hurt that Payton was acting so jealous, but she thought back to Jamari's words. "I'm not taking your place, Payton. You know the varsity team is low on subs. It just seems obvious that Coach would have to fill the roster once he had a chance to inspect the JV girls more closely."

Payton still didn't look happy. "I'm not upset about you being on the team. I don't understand why you didn't tell me. We're best friends. I should have been the first to know."

"You're right," Neeka admitted. "Let's forget about it and head to lunch. I'm starved." She took Payton's arm and started walking toward the cafeteria, suddenly remembering how loud her stomach had growled earlier. "Oh my God, the most embarrassing thing happened to me. The quarterback was standing nearby when..."

****

"Hustle, Leigh!" Coach Mike shouted from across the gym. "That ball isn't going to stop itself from touching the floor."

Neeka grunted as she bent her knees low to dig the ball as it was served to her like a torpedo in a war zone. She was good at passing— when the ball floated toward her from high in the air. But when it came flying at her at warp speed and she had to go low to get to it, it put her off balance. "Dig big!" Coach Gina used to yell at her, and Neeka would, but that was before she'd been paired against the varsity girls. Their serves were much more forceful.

"You've gotten too comfortable in your role as a setter with the JV team. You're on my terrain now. I'm not letting you out of the hot spot until you get at least five of those puppies off the floor," Coach Mike shouted. "Don't keep us here all night, Leigh."

These serves weren't puppies. They were a pack of hungry wolves. But Neeka was just as hungry, and she pushed herself hard, soon managing to dig five balls in a row.

Coach Mike blew his whistle, indicating for the girls to switch stations. They were doing a circuit of drills that afternoon. "Gotta round you girls out as players," Coach had grumbled before they began. The better girls on the team led the drills, leaving room for the less experienced girls to improve.

"Nice work," Annette said as Neeka joined her for the peppering drill. Serve. Pass. Hit. Neeka knew it well. Coach Gina favored it as the JV warm up routine. It was easier than the firing squad she'd just been under.

"Really? I was at that station for ages," Neeka said, flawlessly serving the ball to Annette.

"But not as long as some," Annette replied. "You've got game."

Seeing how Annette had turned on Payton, Neeka didn't take anything the senior said too seriously. She knew she was being buttered up, just as much as she knew that if she let them down, she'd be nothing to Annette. Just another JV player that hadn't improved fast enough.

Focusing on the drill, Neeka grew tired, knowing her muscles would be sore the next day. Coach Mike was pushing the girls hard. She'd been prepared for a long practice, but the intensity of it was incredible. No wonder the varsity team was undefeated so far. The last match they'd lost had been at camp.

The sound of two consecutive whistles echoed across the gym. Neeka wasn't sure what it meant until all the girls gathered around Coach near the net. They were finished with the circuit and moving on. Payton glanced at Neeka and smiled, but said nothing. She'd been quiet all practice, but that was nothing new for Payton. Not since high school had started.

"It's critical you know how to defend your side of the court, but that's no excuse not to attack every opportunity you get. Points don't score themselves. You can't rely on the other team messing up. You have to earn your victory. Fight for it. It's called a kill shot for a reason."

"Yeah!" a few of the girls shouted.

"Line-up. We're not going home tonight until I see you flatten these balls with your kill shots. Make it impossible for the other team to return the message." He pointed to the ball cart. "Annette will divide you in half. Neeka, you'll set on the weak side of the court. Lacey, you'll set strong side. We'll rotate between striking and blocking. When your half isn't on the attack, don't play it easy. Jump high to block. Make the other half work for their points."

Neeka walked over to the right-hand side of the net, called the weak side because it favored the opposing team, whose attacks would likely mostly all be right-handed. She waited while Annette split the team in half, mixing up their skill level. To Neeka's dismay, she sent Payton to Lacey's side.

Payton may not be a superb volleyball player yet, but one thing she was good at was blocking. From her ready position, she could jump higher than most the girls could strike the ball. And her quick footwork meant she could meet the ball just about anywhere. As Neeka's side was chosen to strike first, Payton lined up at the net, an increasingly rare confidence about her.

Thatta girl, Neeka secretly applauded.

Annette passed Neeka a ball. As always, it floated toward her in slow motion. She positioned herself underneath it, squaring her body with the first girl to hit. She didn't see how successful the strike was. Instead, she prepared as Annette sent another ball her way. Neeka felt as if she were moving to a lingering, rhythmic dance. She wasn't just playing volleyball. She was putting on a performance.

"Somebody wants that varsity uniform!" Coach Mike called out.

****

The rest of the team practices that week carried on in a similar fashion. Neeka was doing well, and she knew it. It wasn't just the brilliant smiles form Annette or the occasional compliment from

Coach. Neeka could instinctively feel how well she was doing. When she set, it was if she were in perfect alignment with the universe, as if all the noise and movement of the stars and planets above hushed, waiting for her to make a move.

It was hard to stay focused, especially when she was excited by how well she was doing, but volleyball very much required concentration, no matter how fast the ball was spinning around the court. The principles that she'd learned in basketball, particularly *React, don't think*, didn't apply to volleyball. Yes, she needed to shuffle quickly, but the flow of the game was much smoother, based as much on intelligence as pure effort.

By the end of the week, she shared time with Lacey as primary setter, though she still wasn't officially on the team yet. Lacey seemed to welcome the challenge, much to Neeka's relief. She wouldn't back down from doing her best, but she didn't want her promotion at practice to ruin her growing friendship with the junior.

It's not like Payton is acting like much of a friend these days.

From what Neeka could only assume was jealousy, the better Neeka did, the less Payton spoke with her during practice. But it wasn't just Neeka she was neglecting. From what she could tell, Payton wasn't making an effort with anyone. She was slacking off. While waiting for her turn in-between drills, she didn't pay attention to her teammates or anything that was happening in front of her. Instead, she would fold her arms and rock back and forth, staring around the gym, obviously lost in her own world.

Volleyball was not a solo act. It frustrated Neeka to see Payton act this way, especially as she grew more and more loyal to the varsity team. Though it'd only been a few weeks since the start of school, they were well into the volleyball season now. Volleyball only lasted two months. Payton should be pushing herself harder, using every second of practice to her advantage. But it was as if she'd given up and stopped trying. The whole team felt it, moaning every time Payton made a mistake.

"So much for being a star athlete," one of the girls mumbled when Payton passed a ball straight up to the gym ceiling.

Up until a month ago, Neeka would have defended her friend, but there was nothing she could do. Payton had brought it upon herself by not taking the game more seriously.

At least in basketball, I would shoot hoops with Jamari every night, Neeka thought.

But though she was as frustrated as the other girls, Neeka also worried about Payton. Her behavior wasn't normal. After the final drill of the day, Neeka called Payton over to the bleachers, letting the rest of the team file into the locker room ahead of them.

"Are you okay?" she asked Payton. "I'm worried about you, girl."

Payton took it as an insult. "I don't know what you mean."

"It just seems like you're distracted, that's all," Neeka stated.

"Well, I'm fine," Payton replied before storming to the locker room.

Why are you being this way!? Neeka wanted to shout after her, but didn't. Seriously, what was Payton's problem? Payton was changing, and not for the better.

Recovering from her brief exchange with Payton, Neeka sat on the bleachers, letting her thoughts run wild. She imagined the walls of Hickory Academy turning into a giant Olympic stadium, and Neeka stood on the court, wearing the colors of the US women's team. Fans cheered, little girls looked up to her, and news anchors called out her name.

She must have been lost in the daydream for a while, because when she came to, the gym was empty, as was the locker room when she entered. If she didn't hurry, she'd miss the activity bus home. She rushed to her locker, but froze when she opened the door.

Inside hung a varsity jersey.

CHAPTER 9

A girl with fake blood dripping down her neck walked by Payton as she and Neeka headed toward Biology. They weren't talking much, but the distance forming between them was hardly noticeable in the electric atmosphere that surrounded them. There was a buzz around Hickory Academy. It was the first spirit week of the year, a ritual at the school to garner interest in student activities. Each day had a different theme. Today was labeled Nightmare on Hickory Street and was hosted by the drama department. One of few times throughout the year they were allowed to ditch their school uniforms, half the student body was dressed in ghoulish outfits, from a rotting mummy to a ghost cowgirl.

"Care to join me in the afterlife?" The mummy proposed to Neeka, wrapping a strip of what looked like a dirty washcloth around her wrist.

"Care to feel my shoe in your face?" Neeka asked in reply.

"Feisty," the mummy said with good humor and clomped away to annoy the next set of girls.

Payton laughed. She was in a great mood, and not just because of the homecoming festivities. She hugged her Titans notebook close to her heart. In a few days, she'd be heading to Cincinnati for the weekend to spend some time with her dad. It meant she would miss the Welcome Dance, but she didn't care. With the exception of thinking Dr. B was cute, she wasn't really interested in any of the boys. She had more important things on her mind these days.

"Too bad we have to wear our volleyball hoodies all week. I would love to have dressed up," Payton said to Neeka, trying to make conversation as they continued to push past their haunted classmates. The halls were extra crowded that morning. No one wanted to go to class, each comparing their costumes to see whose was more gruesome.

"I prefer the hoodie," Neeka said, almost defensively.

Payton ignored her tone, knowing Neeka was sensitive when it came to volleyball. Not that Payton talked much about it. The way she'd been playing, volleyball was the last thing she wanted to discuss. But that didn't stop her thinking about it constantly. Her poor performance ate away at her. Try as hard as she did to push volleyball from her mind, it always made its way back into her thoughts. Sometimes, it was all she could think about.

She didn't want her dad to know how bad it was, but she knew she needed his help. She was hoping he'd train with her this weekend up in Cincinnati. For once, she was glad her parents weren't on speaking terms, except when it came to arranging her visits. Otherwise, her mom would have told him by now what a terrible volleyball player their daughter was. She and her mom never discussed volleyball at home, but her mom had been to most of her varsity matches, considering them social time with Lawanda, Neeka's mother. She'd seen with her own two eyes the mess that was Payton Moore on the volleyball court.

Selina ran up to them. Though wearing her hoodie, her face was painted white and she had a trail of fake blood running down her cheek, as if a single red tear had fallen.

For some reason, Neeka tensed beside her when Selina arrived. Payton wasn't sure why.

"Awesome make-up," Payton marveled, wishing she'd thought of doing the same. She had some great face paints at home, ready to be used when Halloween arrived next month.

"This is great, isn't it? We never did anything like this in middle school." Selina paused to adjust her plastic vampire fangs. "Speaking of middle school, you won't believe this, but Valerie Sutton has been snooping around our JV practices this week. She's trying to get in good with Coach Gina. I think she has her eye on JV captain next year."

"Good luck with that," Neeka scoffed, rolling her eyes.

"Well, you don't have to worry about it now that you're also on varsity, Neeka. They probably won't even need you on JV anymore. You're precious goods. Coach wouldn't risk you getting injured. There's a rumor circulating that you're going to replace Lacey in the starting lineup."

Payton stopped in her tracks. Neeka had made varsity? Selina must be mistaken. She had no doubt it was only a matter of time before Neeka did make the team; she was killing at practice, but she would have told her if Coach Mike had officially added her to the roster. She knew how upset Payton had been when she'd held back from her before.

"I better get to class. See you two at lunch," Selina said then turned away, just as the warning bell rang.

"What's happening, Neeka? Are you on varsity?" Payton asked, deciding to be straightforward. There was no point beating around the bush.

"Yes," Neeka admitted quietly. Neeka never spoke quietly.

Payton wasn't sure how she felt. She was obviously happy for her friend, but she was hurt that, for the second time, she had been the last to know Neeka's good news. It worried her. She was afraid her friend was getting too close to the other varsity girls and would soon start ignoring her, like the rest of the team did. It's not like they were growing closer. Volleyball was tearing them apart. So she said nothing, wishing she'd never begged Neeka to come to volleyball camp with her.

"Listen, I just got the news myself. I haven't had time to tell anyone," Neeka tried to explain, the silence between them awkward, but Payton knew she was lying. Her friend rarely lied; she was too outspoken for that, so it was a dead giveaway when she tried.

"Selina knew," was all Payton said.

* * * * * * * * * * * * * * * * * *

In Biology, the students covered their mouths with their sleeves, gagging as what seemed like thousands of fruit flies circled around the classroom. A few had escaped from their vials, multiplying into many. It was an infestation. Hadn't Dr. B said the females laid like five hundred eggs a week? Disgusting!

"Today is supposed to be Nightmare on Hickory Street, not Attack of the Killer Fruit Flies," one of the boys complained.

Dr. B didn't seem at all phased by the swarm of tiny insects. As he talked about his plans for Parents' Night that evening, he casually brushed the flies away as they landed on his glasses. "I'm going to put your parents in your seats, literally," he said. "They'll be conducting the same experiment you did earlier on the fruit flies."

"My dad's going to love that!" Rose snickered. "He's a germ-a-phobe. I can just see him pushing little flies around. He'll probably faint, then sanitize the whole room afterwards. Or he'll just run away. I suddenly like genetic mutation a whole lot more!"

"Forget mutation, what about extermination?" a boy asked, swatting a fly off his nose.

"To be a fly on the wall," Dr. B mused.

It was impossible to tell if he was joking or not, but Payton smiled. She was glad her mom would finally get to meet Dr. B. He was her favorite teacher. Most of the kids hated him, and there was no denying he was a bit of a bore, but she liked him. Though soft-spoken, he was tough, but he wasn't patronizing, not like a lot of the other teachers at the school. She found his soft-spoken authority quite charming. As Dr. B wrote down notes on the whiteboard, Payton realized he wasn't just her favorite teacher—she liked him. Really liked him.

Oh no! I have a crush on my teacher! she exclaimed to herself. She was sitting in a classroom full of boys her age, and all she could think about was the young British professor at the front of the room.

Actually, she guessed it made sense. Look at TV. Nerds were hot at the moment, especially foreign ones. She knew he was too old for her, but she was glad he was too young for her mom. The last thing she wanted to hear when her mom got home from Parents' Night was that she had a date with Payton's teacher.

She was about to ask Neeka if she could borrow a red pen for her notes, but then she remembered she wasn't talking to Neeka. She could forgive Neeka for not coming to her first when she had good news about the varsity team, but she couldn't forgive her a second time. Not straight away.

What was Neeka's problem? Why was she pulling away from her? Everything Payton did, Neeka found fault in it. She could barely breathe the word volleyball without Neeka getting defensive. It wasn't right.

She's obsessed with volleyball, Payton decided. *So much so that she'll do anything to be friends with the other varsity girls, even if it means pushing me out to fit in.* It was the only reason Payton could find to explain why Neeka had refused to tell her about making varsity. She had other friends to share good news with now.

So much for teamsmanship.

* * * * * * * * * * * * * * * * * * *

"Honey, I'm home," Allison announced as she came in through the front door.

Payton was in her room doing her homework. She wanted to catch up on all her assignments before Cincinnati that weekend. That way, nothing would distract her from spending time with her dad. Her screensaver—a photo of her and Neeka at basketball camp together— flashed as she shut down her new computer.

Neeka wouldn't be joining her in Cincinnati. She didn't want to miss the varsity match on Saturday. Payton, on the other hand, didn't mind. It was only a scrimmage. It didn't count toward the season. Even Coach Mike didn't seem to mind, and not just because she'd been playing so badly. He'd been extremely understanding when she'd visited his office to explain the situation. "I have two little tykes of my own, a boy and girl. Dads need to see their kids. I get it. Don't worry," he said, tossing a paper ball into a recycling bin. After a moment, he added, "But if he wants to see you during the championships, tell him he'll have to be the one to giddy up his way down here. I need my entire team on board. You're the best blocker I have."

Payton clung to that compliment. She was more convinced than ever to have her father help her out over the weekend. It would be hard admitting to him how bad she was doing, but he'd know what to do to ensure she got nothing but compliments from Coach Mike from here on out.

****

She reminisced about how, when she was five or six, her dad had taught her tennis for the first time. It took a good few years before she was able to hit the ball over the net, her tiny fists barely able to grip the racket at first. Her dad always told her it was just because she was little, but maybe there was more to it than that. Either way, she had turned into a championship player, one of the best in the state. Just as she had done then, with a bit of support from her dad, she would improve.

So maybe it was a good thing Neeka wasn't coming. That way, Payton had more time alone with her dad. They could practice, and she'd come back the All Star she knew she could be. Soon, she would rule the court.

She set aside all thoughts of volleyball and went to join her mom in the kitchen. "How was it?" Payton asked when she made it downstairs. "Learn anything new about fruit flies?"

"Umm…. It was pretty okay," her mom responded, picking a tiny piece of lint off her skirt. Something was bothering her. It didn't take a genius to tell.

"My mommy radar is on full drive. What's up?"

Taking a mug from the cupboard, her mom prepared to make herself a cup of coffee. She looked tired. "One of your teachers pulled me aside. Ronald Beamon."

Payton was so used to referring to him as Dr. B, it took her a moment to realize what teacher her mom was referring to. "What did he say?" Payton asked.

Whatever it was, it wasn't good. Her mom seemed troubled. She couldn't imagine why. She was getting good grades. He had said so himself. Her throat closed up when she suddenly thought back to the day he had asked her if anything was wrong.

"He was worried about you. It seems you've been quite distant in class these last few weeks. He thinks something is troubling you. Is there something troubling you, baby?" Her mom looked at her meaningfully before she returned to pouring her coffee.

"No," Payton spat, knowing her mom would only think she was being silly if she knew she couldn't get volleyball off her mind. She might even make her quit the team. Though Payton was miserable, she wasn't a quitter. She could only imagine what her dad would think if she left the team after being given the opportunity to play varsity her freshman year. "Why in the hillbillies (is this a word that teenagers would say?) would he say that?"

"He says you aren't talking with Neeka as much. You seem tense all the time, not as fresh-faced and eager as most freshman are their first few weeks of high school." She paused, hesitating. "He thinks it has something to do with volleyball."

"Well, he's wrong," Payton said defensively, unable to admit the truth.

Her mom could read her like a book. "Payton, it's just volleyball," she persisted. "If it is becoming a burden, you don't have to play. There are millions of other activities you can be doing. You're young. You need to be enjoying life, not putting yourself under unnecessary pressure—"

"I said he's wrong!" Payton exclaimed, interrupting her mom's pep talk. Her mother would never understand. All Stars did not quit.

Realizing she was living up to the image Dr. B had painted of her, she softened her voice. "It's not volleyball," she lied. "High school is just a bit overwhelming, that's all. I don't know how Dr. B can talk. He's partially to blame. He treats us like college students when we're only freshman. It's a lot to take in."

Allison considered this and dropped the subject. Payton returned to her room, fuming. She had intended to finish up her homework for the week, but she couldn't think. How dare Dr. B! Why was he so obsessed? He had no right to interfere with her life. If her mom had decided to make her quit, he could have cost her a spot on the varsity team.

In tears at Dr. B's intrusion into her personal affairs, Payton reached for her cell phone to call Neeka, but stopped, remembering the day Neeka had pulled her aside after practice to ask if everything was okay. Neeka would probably side with Dr. B. Unable to face any further betrayal that night, Payton cuddled into her comforter and fell asleep.

****

The next morning, as she prepared for school, Payton was still so angry at Dr. B., she could barely look at him in Biology. In her mind, she kept willing the fruit flies to attack him, though half their population had died off due to double-sided tape that had been hung from the ceiling. Rumor had it one of the parents the night before had threatened to have the biology lab shut down if the fly problem wasn't taken care of.

Payton carried her anger with her throughout the rest of her morning classes. The theme that day was Back to the Seventies, the result of creative planning by the technology club. Colorful peace signs were stuck around the classrooms and the jeans of choice had flared legs and bell bottoms. Kids kept referring to each other as groovy and rad. It was amusing, but not enough to quiet Payton's spirits. By lunch, she knew she had to confront Dr. B.

As she stormed toward the biology lab, her heart pounded in her chest. She had never stood up to a teacher before, but she refused to let her courage drop. She didn't hate him. In fact, she still had a bit of a crush on him, but as far as she was concerned, he was now the opposing team.

"Good day, Payton," he greeted when she entered the room. He was sitting at his desk eating a chicken sandwich. "Did you leave something behind after first period?"

"You know why I'm here," she said, her voice raising an octave. "Why did you say that to my mom last night? What right do you have?" She felt as if all the frustration she'd felt the last few weeks was pouring out of her.

He put down his sandwich and let her vent. When she was done, he said very gently, "I think the reason you are so upset is because I am correct in my judgment of the matter. Volleyball is stressing you out. You've spent so much time carrying this burden around by yourself, it is a shock to you to have to be confronted with it by others."

Payton was speechless. Reluctant tears threatened to cascade down her cheeks. She sniffed, unable to form a reply.

"You're a good student, Payton," Dr. B stated. "It's quite clear that I support strong academics and expect my students to stay focused when I'm lecturing, but I also believe academics can be enjoyable for youths. It's why I fill my syllabus with hands-on experiments. Kids your age are meant to be having fun, but I have seen no joy in your face since your first varsity match. You seem as if you're holding your breath all the time. I can't help but wonder if, when it comes to volleyball, you're a fish out of water, struggling to survive."

Payton looked away, collecting herself, then met Dr. B's gaze. "I am," she admitted. It was a relief to do so. Somehow, she felt a portion of the weight lift off her shoulders, but only a small bit.

"Is volleyball worth it?" he inquired unassumingly, allowing her the freedom to answer as she chose.

"Yes. It's worth the struggle. I've been good at every sport I've tried. I know the volleyball season is short, but it's still early days for me. I've only just started playing, compared to the other girls on the team. I can't quit yet. I have to keep trying, for myself and for my team. They believed in me. I've let them down so far, but I can't give up. You only really fail if you quit."

"Those are brave words, Payton, but not necessarily wise. It's okay to call time on something if you're doing it for the wrong reasons, such as to please others without acknowledging your own feelings." When she didn't respond, he changed directions. "Was it not you who introduced Neeka to volleyball?"

How did he know that? Payton wondered.

Reading her expression, he answered, "I would hear you two talking about practice incessantly when school first started."

Oh.

"Neeka seems to be doing well," he reflected. "Could you not consider your duty to your team fulfilled knowing you recruited one of their best players? She's on the team because you encouraged her to be."

Payton had never thought of it that way, but it was irrelevant. Yes, there were times she wanted to quit, and Dr. B had just given her an easy excuse to do so, but she wanted to prove to herself as much as she did to the others that she could improve. She could be a star athlete, either through natural ability or perseverance and hard work.

"I'm not walking way," she insisted.

Dr. B nodded, accepting her resolve. "Then may I suggest you take a new approach. Don't stress yourself out trying to be all things to all people. Break it down. Think of it as looking at volleyball through a microscope. Pick one thing to perfect, something you feel you already have a natural ability for, then move on from there."

"You mean specialize? I already have. I'm the middle hitter and blocker, starting lineup for JV and whenever Coach Mike subs me in for varsity. It's an important position. I'm central to both the offensive and defensive strategies of the team."

"And you feel you have to be excellent in that position?"

"Of course," Payton said indignantly.

"I'm not saying you won't eventually be, but what about breaking it down even further than what position you play. Find something very specific to improve upon."

Used to being an all-round great player, she was resistant to the idea. Dr. B could sense this. "Not permanently. Just choose one thing to work on for now. Take it one step at a time and build from there. Be a master of one thing, and soon you'll be a master of all things."

Without meaning to, he sounded like the old guy from the *Karate Kid* movies her dad had made her watch. Too bad Dr. B couldn't also catch flies. Then all their problems would be solved.

Payton thought about it. His words made sense. Perhaps her

problem wasn't a lack of ability. Maybe it was trying to master too many things at once, like throwing all her firewood into one messy pile without stacking it neatly.

"Okay," she said. "I'll try not to stress so much. Thank you, Dr. B," she said. "I'll let you get back to your lunch now."

Walking toward the cafeteria, admiring the hundreds of peace signs on the walls, she was finally beginning to feel some sense of peace inside her own self. She just wished Dr. B hadn't said anything to her mom. His behavior was confusing. Didn't he have anything better to do than meddle in his students' personal lives?

Still, she was grateful for his advice. It seemed wise. She just wasn't sure what she was going to do with it.

CHAPTER 10

"Mine!" Selina yelled, diving for the ball from behind the ten-foot line. These days, that was her favorite word. She hogged the ball every chance she got, whether she was passing or striking. Not great etiquette in volleyball, but it got results. Selina passed the ball to Neeka, who set it for Payton. Willing her body and mind to join forces, Payton drew her right hand back and pounded the ball with her palm, hoping it hit the unguarded floor she was trying to aim for.

It did. The point went to Hickory Academy.

Trying to keep her focus, Payton didn't celebrate between serves. Instead, she went straight back into her ready position. She saw Neeka give her a thumbs up out of the corner of her eye, but she pretended not to notice. They were talking again. Payton decided to forgive her for being so secretive, but she still didn't feel completely confident in their friendship. But that's not why she ignored Neeka just then. She had to concentrate. She didn't want to leave room for any doubt to invade. Doubt multiplied faster than fruit flies, and when it attacked, there was little she could do to regain her composure.

They were in their final set. Hickory Academy had a strong lead, but their competition wasn't fierce. The Brenton Cougars were only in their first season. She almost felt bad for the girls. She knew what they were going through. It was hard putting yourself out there when you knew you were destined to do poorly, but that didn't mean you stopped trying.

After a short rally, Payton blocked their spike, sending the ball to the floor on the other side of the net. Hickory Academy's next serve went straight to the floor—an ace.

Normally, Coach Gina would have subbed her out by now, but Payton had scheduled a brief conversation with the woman upon her return from Cincinnati, asking for more opportunities to play. Coach Gina was more than willing to give her extra playing time, allowing her to "work out the kinks" as she'd put it, a proud smile upon her face. "You've got an eternal fire in you, Payton," she'd said. "You're an inspiration."

They were kind words, though not wholly accurate. Payton was performing better at JV matches, but she owed a lot of the credit to her athleticism. She had more strength and endurance than most girls her age. Too bad she couldn't say the same for the varsity girls.

At the varsity matches, she was managing to get the ball over the net when she hit, but she had no direction in her aim. It flew wildly. One time, she'd even heard the hitters on the other team yell, "Free!" The problem was, it hadn't been a free ball—one that is passed leisurely over the net because there was no opportunity for a strong attack. It had been an attack! But a very, very poor one.

From the sidelines, Coach Mike had given up critiquing her. Instead, he would drop his head and mutter, "Come on, come on," when she messed up. She remembered the time he had kicked a chair when she'd nearly cost them a match. At least he wasn't throwing furniture around, but it still wasn't enough. She wanted to earn his praise.

"Mine!" Selina yelled again when the ball came their way. She went for a back row strike and succeeded. Running to Neeka, the two girls high-fived each other as the scoreboard changed. Watching Selina and Neeka, a realization suddenly hit her. Payton and Neeka hadn't hugged on the court since Neeka had been promoted to varsity. They had grown extremely distant, though they still managed small conversations in Biology.

When the match ended, the victory going to Hickory Academy, Selina skipped up to Payton at the bench, an unfaltering smile on her face. "Did you hear the news?" she asked, taking a huge gulp of water from Payton's water bottle.

"Well, it's obviously not that you found your own water bottle." Payton was used to being the last to hear good news these days, but she entertained Selina, knowing the news must be momentous if a genuine smile replaced Selina's usual smirk. "What news?"

"Starting next week, I'm practicing with varsity! First you, then Neeka, now me! Newbies unite! They obviously didn't know how good they had it when we signed up."

Payton's face fell. "You are?"

Selina rolled her eyes. "Oh toughen up, Moore. Don't be so sensitive. If you're worried about your spot on the team, work harder. That's my philosophy."

I am working hard! Payton wanted to shout. Instead, she patted Selina on the back. "You're right. Sorry. It'll be great. I can't wait."

"We'll be bench buddies," Selina said.

That's what Neeka had said, but her behind had seen very little of the bench recently.

"Yeah," Payton said weakly.

As Selina moved on to the next girl to share her good news with, Payton suddenly regretted her last-minute decision in Cincinnati not to let her dad know the truth about how much she needed his help. They'd had a totally amazing weekend. On the drive up, they'd stopped for cheese and pretzels. A white long-tailed deer had nearly jumped in front of them on the highway as they neared Cincinnati. Her dad had said it was a good omen for the Titans, and sure enough, they won the game on Sunday. She'd had a hard time leaving her room in her dad's new apartment. He'd decked it out in sports gear, including an air hockey table.

The only downfall to the weekend was how he kept telling her how proud he was of her. She'd planned on being honest with him about volleyball from the start of the trip, so she could get it over with, but her courage failed her. Then, when her dad introduced her to his doorman as, "This is my daughter Payton. She's a real champ. She made varsity her freshman year," she lost all hope of saying anything to her dad. She didn't want to ruin their time together or embarrass him in front of his friends.

They wouldn't have had a lot of time to practice, anyway, she'd told herself. Her dad had planned a busy weekend. Pizza late Friday night. Hiking on Saturday morning. Swimming in the afternoon. A football match with root beer floats in the evening. And then the Titans game on Sunday. She'd refused to close her eyes on the car ride home, not wanting to miss a moment with her dad, but she'd been so tired, so didn't remember her head hitting her pillow when she was finally back in Nashville.

Payton watched as her teammates congratulated Neeka on a great game. Finally, they'd won again! It was a great boost to their morale after their losing streak. No one could deny that Neeka had played a huge role in their victory. She made it easy for the hitters to find good target space.

She thought of Dr. B's advice to pick one thing to master. Neeka had taken control of setting. She'd built upon her strength—her analytical approach to the game. It had worked in her favor. Payton could do the same. She just had to get creative and think of something about herself that could be developed into a superstar skill.

****

Demonbreun High, the defending District Champions.

The girls on the team looked like college players, and that was just the JV team. It was intermission before the varsity match. JV had already played and been annihilated. How could they compete? The Demonbreun High girls were tall, toned, and lean. Everything about them screamed professionals. They weren't rude or catty; they were focused. Eerily focused. It was almost scary. Payton would have felt better if they had been hollering insults at them. Instead, they just zoned into the game, like robot volleyball players from another dimension.

Selina and Payton were barely used during the JV match, and Neeka not at all. As a result, the scoreboard was an embarrassment, but it was a sacrifice Coach Mike was willing to make. It was obvious the Hickory Academy JV team would win no championship this year. Varsity, however, was wiping away the competition one by one. They weren't sure how they'd fare against Demonbreun High, but Coach Mike didn't want to risk any of them getting injured during what he considered a useless JV match.

The bleachers were quickly becoming a tidal wave of loud, obnoxious fans smothered in black and yellow and blue and green. Both Demonbreun High and Hickory Academy were undefeated. Droves had turned out to witness their rivalry. A group of boys had come dressed in aquamarine tutus and blonde wigs, raising money for a local charity. Cheerleaders stretched near the sidelines, though Coach Gina had them all beat in her enthusiasm. Even a local sports journalist had come to take notes, despite the fact this wasn't a championship match.

Not yet, Payton predicted.

She was nervous, but she knew she was nowhere close to how Neeka felt, replacing Lacey as setter in the starting lineup. New to the spotlight, Neeka didn't have the same experience Payton did when it came to playing under the pressure of a full house, knowing the team was counting on you, along with hundreds of fans. Neeka kept clenching and unclenching her fists, pacing while Coach Mike threw a pep talk at her.

"Those uniforms are hideous," Selina said, commenting on the yellow and black Demonbreun High jerseys. "They look like overgrown bumblebees."

"Or wasps," Payton said, never one to underestimate the competition.

The referee blew his whistle, and all the formalities that were required at the start of a match, began. The national anthem played. Hands were shaken. Fans took out their handcrafted signs and began hollering. The scoreboard lights lit up.

Lacey took her seat on the bench next to Payton and Selina. Payton felt awful for her. It was one thing to be a sub from the start, but it was another to have your position on the starting lineup taken away. It wasn't Neeka's fault, but Payton couldn't help but feel a wrong had been committed, especially since Lacey was so nice. She didn't deserve to be cast aside.

She seemed to be handling it well enough, though. When the first set began, Lacey clapped and cheered as Hickory Academy and Demonbreun High engaged in a never-ending rally. "That's it, Annette!" she yelled. "Come on, girls. Keep it together!" But though she put on a brave face, Payton noticed a tension in Lacey's posture whenever Neeka set the ball.

She caught Payton's pitying glances. "I know I'm a good player," she said confidently. "Neeka is just better. I'm okay with that."

"You're a better person than I would be," Selina confessed, overhearing their conversation. "I love Neeka, she's my girl, but I would put pepper in her eye if she'd stolen my spot. I'm ruthless like that."

"She didn't steal it; she earned it," Lacey objected, but the remorse in her eyes didn't completely match her conviction.

Demonbreun High took an early lead, as expected. The fans in black and yellow were confident, used to winning, but Hickory Academy soon took over, causing the fans in blue and green to riot. There would be no clear favorite for this match. Either team could take home the prize. Though no trophy was on offer that night, respect and pride were greater rewards.

It was a tough ride. Girls threw themselves at the ground to dig the ball. Serves left bruises on unsuspecting players. For the first time, Neeka had to back set, blindly delivering the ball to a hitter standing behind her without turning her body. But Hickory Academy was able to maintain their lead, winning both the first and second sets. In response, the Demonbreun High girls began to show a bit of emotion, their rage evident.

Selina was as wild as the fans in the bleachers. She clapped and hollered, her voice running hoarse by the end of the second set. Payton wished she could be more like Selina, but what she really wanted was to be the one in the court earning all the glory. It wasn't jealousy—more like quiet admiration. It was the same way she felt when she went to a WNBA game. She wanted to be in the middle of the action.

As *libero*, Annette was all over the back court. Her and Neeka were an unstoppable pair as they assisted the hitters to score over and over again. Neeka was flawless. She owned it, like she was an essential part of game, as much as the net and ball. She belonged there. No matter how nervous she was, she had poise. Never out of position, she knew exactly where she was supposed to be and got the ball where it needed to go.

If Payton was a fish out of water when it came to volleyball, Neeka was the sea itself, graceful but dangerous.

It was a far cry from basketball camp only a couple of months earlier, when Neeka had fumbled around the court as though she had two left feet. At times in basketball, she looked as if she were afraid to receive the ball. Now, she was fearless, with the power of a lioness but the elegance of a swan.

How can she be so good and I'm so terrible? Payton thought. *Didn't it go against some law of science or something?* For Neeka, it was a miracle. For Payton, it was the exact opposite. An anti-miracle.

Lacey must have sensed her unhappiness. She patted Payton on the knee, but said nothing. A silent camaraderie was forming between them. No matter what Lacey said, Payton knew it must be hard for her to watch Neeka doing so well. Every time the team scored a point, they briefly huddled on the court, patting Neeka enthusiastically on the back, along with the hitter she had assisted. And every time, Payton heard Lacey let out a small, secret sigh.

****

Hickory Academy won their third set in a row, taking home the match. The Hickory Academy fans went ballistic as the Demonbreun High folks stormed home. Blue glitter sprinkled down around them. They had stolen Demonbreun High's perfect record. Now, they were the only undefeated team in the district this year.

Payton had played briefly, as had Lacey and the other substitute hitter, but since only three sets had been needed to triumph, the starting lineup had mostly seen the match through until the end. It was fortunate. Her five minutes pitted against Demonbreun High was enough for one night. She had a lot of work to do if she wanted to feel even remotely confident by the next time they played them. It was inevitable that the two teams would meet again.

Nearby, the sports journalist interviewed Annette. "How do you feel being captain of an undefeated team?" she asked.

"Like a rock star," Annette replied, drinking up the attention.

Payton couldn't blame her. She'd been captain of a winning team before, and with hope, she would be again come basketball season. It did feel like being a rock star.

"Great blocking," Coach Gina complimented her. "For once, you weren't the tallest girl on the court, but you still did a wonderful job."

Payton thanked Coach Gina then sat down on the bench, taking a small moment for herself. She watched as Neeka skipped up the bleachers to her family. Mr. Leigh had finally made it to the match. They hadn't spent much time together since Neeka was put in the starting lineup, but despite the difficulties in their friendship as of late, Payton was happy for Neeka. She knew how much her dad's presence meant to her, especially since this was the biggest match of the season so far. Watching Mr. Leigh take Neeka into his arms, Payton knew it was time she called her own dad. She couldn't let her fear of failure rule her anymore. If she wanted to do better, she would have to face her fears head on.

"I'm ready," she said aloud.

"Ready for what?" her mom asked, joining her.

"I need dad's help," Payton admitted.

Allison put her arm around her daughter. Suddenly feeling emotional, Payton was grateful. She sank her head into her mom's shoulder, tears starting to form.

"I hate to admit it, honey, but I think you do. This is something your dad is best at," she said, rubbing Payton's head as her daughter began to sob.

****

As soon as she got home, Payton ran upstairs and called her dad. The phone rang for ages, but she refused to hang up, knowing her dad never missed her calls. He'd answer. No more excuses or self-pity. If she was going to improve, she needed help. The same help her dad had provided her all the years of her childhood. He was as much a part of this as she was.

"Hi baby gir—"

"Don't say anything," she pleaded the second he picked up. "Dad, I haven't been completely honest with you. I'm terrible at volleyball. I mean, really bad. I'm the worst girl on the team. The other girls had high hopes for me, and I'm letting them down to the point they barely speak to me. I need you, Dad. You and I are a team, and I'm calling an emergency team meeting." She stopped, breathless, and twisted the phone cord around her arm as she waited for his reply.

Her dad said nothing at first. It killed her. But he finally responded, "I can't leave just yet, but I'll come as soon as I can."

Payton's heart sank, almost to the point of tears again. "But Dad—"

"Darling, listen." This time he interrupted her. "I would leave this minute, if I could. But I have responsibilities at work I can't neglect. You come first, baby, but I know you'll be all right until I get there. I believe in you."

He believes in me? Did he hear anything I just said?

Payton's dad cleared his throat. Was he getting weepy? Her dad didn't cry, not when it came to sports. "Payton, I watched as you kicked your first soccer ball and beat me for the first time at table tennis. I have seen you win trophies and All Star games. But today, you have shown you have the heart of a true champion. There's no such thing as a perfect athlete, baby girl. Champions are those who can recognize their flaws and use that knowledge to up their game. I'm so proud of you for being honest with me, darling. You earn your Victory wings tonight."

CHAPTER 11

How the mighty do fall.

Practice wasn't the same as usual. The snap, crackle, and pop was gone. While they waited for Coach Mike—who was unusually late—to arrive, most of the varsity girls stood alone, sulking. Even Annette looked defeated, rubbing her fingers against her temples. No one spoke. There was no bubbly chatter or exciting reply of their latest victory.

That was because there was no latest victory.

We haven't hit a wall. We've hit a fortress, Neeka thought, setting the ball halfheartedly against the side of the gym wall.

Hickory Academy was no longer undefeated. They'd lost three games in a row. They'd been flying so high after beating Demonbreun, but now they had hit the ground hard. In sports, no one was invincible, a fact they had learned the hard way. They couldn't point the blame at any one person. They were all performing badly.

Payton came up to Neeka, resting her head again the wall. Neeka was surprised at the casual gesture and stopped the ball. They'd been avoiding each other lately. She wasn't entirely sure why. They weren't mad at each other, but there was a tension between them. They didn't talk the way they used to. When they did speak, like in Biology, it was mostly out of routine. The awkwardness was too exhausting. It was easier just to avoid one another completely.

"It'll be okay," Payton assured her. "We'll recover."

Neeka was about to respond, but Annette, overhearing Payton's words, lifted her head up.

"And what would you know, Payton? You haven't gotten any better. I don't know why Coach keeps you on the team. I made a mistake asking you to join. I had so much confidence in you, but I was wrong. I should have been out looking for someone better."

"Don't take this out on her," Neeka snapped. "She's not the problem; we all are."

"Neeka's right," Lacey said. "I think we may have gotten a bit overconfident."

"That's not it," Annette replied. "Overconfidence is never a problem. That's a myth."

"It is if it causes you to get lazy and keep your guard down," another senior said, stepping forward.

"You all calling me lazy?" Annette accused.

"No," the girl said, shaking her head vigorously, frightened.

Lacey put her hand on Annette's shoulder to calm her down. "She's just saying we've all lost our concentration."

That's not all we've lost, Neeka thought. It was true that they had grown overconfident and let their guard down, but they were also no longer working as a team, not at the level they should be. When they weren't lost in their own miserable thoughts, they were bickering with each other, moaning every time someone made the smallest mistake. Neeka wasn't sure they could survive another loss. It might split them up for good.

On second thought, they never had been fully united. The way Payton had been treated over the last few weeks, like she was an outcast, was just a small example of the way the team gossiped about each other and took sides. That was just the beginning. Neeka hated to admit it, but the team had really started to divide the moment she had taken Lacey's spot on the starting lineup. It'd made the girls paranoid, like no one was safe, especially since Selina had officially been put on the varsity roster. In their minds, it'd become a competition of the survival of the fittest. They were more focused on each other than on their opponents.

We can't survive this way, Neeka knew, particularly not in a game that was as heavily orchestrated as volleyball. They needed to get along. Because they were only allowed three moves to get the ball over the net, the team had to act as one force, the way a school of fish turned at the exact same time in the water. They had to think the same, to move the same.

"Where is coach?" she wondered out loud, but no one answered.

Losing those last three matches had been brutal. The first had been to a team they never should have lost too. The second, their worst, had been a rematch against Demonbreun High. Though they'd already suffered one loss, they'd walked into the rematch like they were fearsome cowgirls and this was the Wild West. But the Demonbreun High girls were not intimidated. They'd done their homework. They knew the moves Hickory Academy would make before Hickory Academy did.

It hadn't been an easy victory for Demonbreun High. The score had been close most sets. Both teams had fought hard. Annette nearly injured herself in the clash. As *libero*, it was her responsibility to ensure the balls that came to their side of the net were successfully passed on, but they came at her like Thor with a hammer. She sacrificed her body, diving and rolling to save the ball and keep it in play. The way she rubbed her shoulder after lurching into one of the dives, Neeka suspected Annette had injured herself, but she said nothing, knowing Annette would never forgive her if she gave Coach cause to pull the senior out of even one game.

Because the spikes from Demonbreun High had been difficult for Annette to dig, though she was able to reach them, her passes to Neeka wobbled unsteadily. Neeka had very few opportunities to set the ball properly. As a result, the hitters couldn't perform as well as they had done most of the season. Their chain of play was in a bad need of repair. In volleyball, each link counted.

"Give Neeka something to work with!" Coach Mike had yelled at the back row. "If you can't give Neeka something to work with, then the hitters might as well sit out. We can't win this game on dinks alone. We need kill shots!"

Demonbreun High was ruthless. Hickory Academy had enraged them when they took away their undefeated title for the season, and now they were taking out their vengeance. A lot of the points Hickory Academy did score were not because of their attacks but because of their defensive strategies. In this way, Payton had been one of their biggest assets. She really was a great blocker. Coach Mike spent a lot of the match subbing her in to play the front row, then took her back out before she had a chance to serve. It was their only hope, since the hitters weren't getting very far, not with the way Neeka was setting.

Though they managed to challenge Demonbreun High with frequent rallies that took a long time before someone scored, especially in the final set, it wasn't enough. Demonbreun High won, much to the jubilations of their fans. This time, it was the Hickory Academy fans who left with their heads down, ignoring the banter the Demonbreun High students threw at them.

It would have been easy to excuse a loss against Demonbreun High, Coach even commended them for battling so hard, but then they lost their third match in a row. The final loss had been against the Hawks, who the girls hadn't played since camp. With their experience and momentum, and with Neeka as their secret weapon, a win against the Hawks should have been easy, but they'd lost, and Coach Mike wasn't as forgiving as he had been before.

We'd been as sloppy as a pig in a trough, Neeka thought. *Including me.*

During the match against the Hawks, the ball came flying to their side of the net in relatively easy strikes, at least compared to the Demonbreun High hitters, but Hickory Academy was distracted. Neeka's sets were inaccurate. A couple of the girls made a foot fault, stepping past the end line when they served, resulting in a side-out. Serves also went out of bounds. It was a complete circus, as if they'd been replaced by clones who'd never touched a ball before.

In his speech afterwards, which was anything but peppy, Coach Mike threatened that "changes may have to be made" before slapping down his clipboard and leaving the girls to talk among themselves. It'd been a shock to hear, and the seniors had immediately begun grumbling to each other about how ridiculous their performance was on the court.

"We looked like a bunch of rodeo clowns," one said. "Y'all might as well stick a bright fuzzy nose on me."

"What are we doing wrong?" another whined.

The stakes were highest for the seniors. This was their last season playing for Hickory Academy. All four of them had been on the very first volleyball team the school had organized. They wanted their legacy to shine by bringing home the District Championship trophy, but their current losses pointed the team in the other direction. As the seniors stomped around the locker room, the rest of the team sat silently, thankful no one was pointing any fingers just yet.

Listening to the girls shout at each other now while waiting for Coach Mike to arrive at practice, Neeka couldn't help but wonder if his tardiness meant he was living up to his threat that changes would have to be made. She wasn't sure what he meant by that, but whatever it was, it wasn't good.

****

"Here he is," Lacey said, pointing to the gym doors when Coach Mike finally arrived.

He was followed by Coach Gina and the rest of the JV team. Coach Gina twitched uncomfortably by his side, clearly not in favor of whatever stunt he was about to pull. The woman had never been a fan of hard motivational techniques. She trusted that encouragement pushed the players forward better than fear. Neeka agreed with her to some extent, but she also believed that the moment a coach went soft on the players, the players would go soft on themselves. Sometimes, they needed tough love to keep them driven.

Coach Mike paraded the JV team in front of the varsity players. "They're here to keep you girls on your toes," Coach Mike announced. "I mean that quite literally. Until I see some improvement in your game, until your techniques are back at a competitive level, we're all practicing together. I only want the best of the best on my team. Now, I have a bigger pool to choose from."

Selina looked thwarted, as if her recent promotion to varsity was no longer as valid as it used to be.

"It's just a display to motivate us," Neeka whispered to her. "Get us back on our feet. I doubt Coach will make any more changes to the team."

"Look at Lacey," Selina muttered. "No one is safe."

"Just don't forget these are our teammates too," Neeka reminded her, hoping the break down in teamsmanship that happened with the varsity team didn't trickle down to JV.

Neeka spotted Valerie Sutton among the girls. She'd heard Valerie had started practicing with the JV team at the middle school gym, no doubt after pestering Coach Gina, but she wasn't allowed to compete, not until she entered high school the next year. Where the rest of the JV girls looked distressed, unwilling participants in the stunt because a lot of them were friends with the varsity girls, Valerie was absolutely delighted.

She pushed her auburn hair out of her way. "What are we waiting for?" she hollered. "Let the games begin!"

****

Neeka was never so happy to see the girls' locker room. Practice had been ruthless. The varsity girls had still managed to outperform the JV team, much to their relief, but with most of the girls on edge a majority of the practice, it had been an emotionally daunting task. Annette had never yelled at them so much. Neeka assumed she was trying to make up for Coach Mike's near silence, which was even more unnerving. At least Coach Gina had been supportive, yelling praise at both sides.

"Thank God the JV girls have gone back to the middle school lockers to change. I don't think I could have stood anymore of Valerie Sutton's annoying voice," Selina beefed. "She sounded like a parrot mimicking Annette. What right does she have? She's not even on the team. Not really. Next thing you know, she'll show up at our JV basketball practices. If that happened, I'd have to hire a henchman to send her to Alaska. He'd probably do it for free, just to get her out of the country. I feel sorry for the JV team, putting up with her every day."

We're still JV, Neeka wanted to say, but kept quiet because it wasn't a whole truth. Now that she was starting for varsity, she never played a JV match when it was on the same day as a varsity match, which was quite frequent. Coach Gina had recruited a new sophomore from Memphis to join the JV team. Neeka just assumed the girl was filling her place, ensuring the roster was full.

Feeling dirty with all the dust that had been flying around, Neeka went to the sink to wash the grime from under her nails. She wasn't allowed to have long nails while playing sports. It was a safety hazard. The last thing the district officials wanted was an eye injury due to overgrown nails. So Neeka wasn't able to do much in the manicure department these days, but she did like to keep her nails clean and freshly polished in colorful shades, a glittery midnight blue being her favorite color at the moment, close to the colors of Hickory Academy. She'd even put yellow stars in the middle of each so it they looked like the night sky.

After washing her hands, Neeka splashed cool water against her face. Autumn couldn't get here fast enough. As she headed back toward the locker area, away from the sinks and showers, Annette suddenly blocked her path, her usual way to make an entrance when she wanted to talk to someone.

"What's your problem?" Neeka asked when Annette didn't speak. "You're breathing so loudly, I can barely hear myself think."

"I want to know if you're tough enough to handle this game," Annette stated bluntly, ignoring Neeka's remark. "Because I'm not so sure you are."

Neeka clenched her fist but tried to stay calm. A fight in the locker room was the last thing she wanted. "Get out of my way, Annette. You're being ridiculous. It's not my fault we lost."

Annette refused to move. "I don't think you're taking your spot on varsity seriously," she insisted.

What?! Neeka couldn't believe what she was hearing. She took the game more seriously than most the girls on the team. So much so that she'd committed herself to helping Selina practice after normal practices were finished, even though it interfered with her homework. "I don't know how you can even say that," she countered. "You think I just walked onto the starting lineup? I earned my place on the team."

"I think you made the starting lineup because you had a natural talent, but that's not the same as taking the game seriously. Two losses, and you completely fell apart the last match. We should have beaten the Hawks."

Neeka was fuming. It took all her control not to reach forward and flick Annette across the head. The entire team had been playing badly. She would not be the scapegoat for their three losses.

You're supposed to be leading us. What does that say about you? Neeka desperately wanted to say. But Annette was looking for an argument, someone she could vent her frustrations on. She wanted Neeka to react, knowing she was one to always speak her mind, to never hold back. But Neeka wasn't having that either. Instead, she ignored her impulse to reply with a sarcastic remark and tried to keep a blank face, not showing a trace of emotion.

Needing to get away from Annette as soon as she could, she responded in as calm a voice as possible, "I want to win too. Why do you think I'm trying to lose? It makes no sense. You think I'm some sort of spy or something? Get real."

Annette, having unmistakably prepared for an argument, was taken aback by Neeka's somewhat sensible statement. She was quiet for a moment, but refused to let Neeka pass. Whether she said what she did next out of spite or genuine concern, Neeka wasn't sure, but it nearly put Neeka over the edge.

"You need to work harder, Neeka. Whether you mean to or not, you're slacking off, just like Payton. I know you two are close, like two blue jays in the same tree. If you care about Payton's future on the team, you need to make sure she works harder too. Tell her to stop joking around all the time. The two of you bird brains need to get your act together."

Annette huffed and turned away, leaving Neeka to smolder, like an active volcano about to blow its top.

CHAPTER 12

"I can't believe her. That... That..."

"Neeka," her mom warned her, shooting a disapproving look at her through the rear view mirror. "I didn't raise you to speak using bad language. I won't tolerate it."

Jamari sat in the front of the car, a wide smile on his face, as if daring Neeka to say what she was thinking. "Yeah, Neeka," he mocked.

Jamari's jeep had broken down. He'd tried to start it after his pre-season basketball practice, but the engine wouldn't turn over. Neeka blamed the Gatorade he no doubt used as gas. There were endless bottles of it in the backseat of his car. Since their mom had to drive out to collect him from his magnet school and wait for the tow truck to take his jeep away, she'd passed by Hickory Academy to pick Neeka up after her volleyball practice. Though it meant waiting for ages for the tow truck, Neeka was glad. It meant she could vent her aggravation after Annette's confrontation in the locker room. If she'd taken the activity bus home, she was sure her rage would have rippled throughout Nashville like a supernova.

"We should do this more often," Jamari said. "I'm so used to driving, it's nice to be chauffeured for once." He leaned back in his seat and went to put his legs on the dashboard, but their mom slapped them down.

Lawanda shook her head. "I love you kids, but you all are a handful.

I like the hour of quiet I get after work before you two get home. I need that time to myself. Being a social worker at the hospital is hard. So is being a mom."

"I finally get why you pushed Neeka into basketball all these years when she was so terrible at it," he teased.

"They didn't push me," Neeka said, irritated. "I wanted to play. And I worked hard to improve, because that's what you do when you're on a team. You work hard. I always work hard. I can't believe Annette would try to call me lazy. She's nothing but a lousy…"

"Renika Leigh!" her mom scolded.

Neeka sank in her seat, her arms folded. "I was going to say rat."

"Sure you were, sis." Jamari smirked.

"That's enough of that sort of talk," Lawanda ordered. When their mother was firm about something, she meant it.

"She's a terrible captain," Neeka mumbled. "She's supposed to pull the team together. Instead, she divides everyone. Pushes people into corners."

Her mom turned the corner into their gated middle-income community and entered the security code. "Annette is just frustrated because you've lost three matches in a row after being undefeated. If I were in her shoes, I'd feel the same way. I remember my last year of high school. I wanted our swim team to win a trophy so badly. We didn't come close to the championships. I was so upset, your Memaw made a trophy out of an old coffee mug and gave it to me. It had Number One written in marker on the side. It's still packed away in the attic somewhere."

"That's a nice story, Mom, but Annette is different. She doesn't simply want to win. She's obsessed with it. And that's what is driving the team apart. She knows she'll never have the chance again if she doesn't make her team in college, but she's going about it all the wrong way."

"Deal with it," Jamari said, stretching. "You get all sorts in sports. You were yelled at, so what. Wah wah. Get over it. You said she asked you if you were tough enough. Well, if you want to prove her wrong, toughen up. Shake it off. Move on."

"Has anyone ever told you how unhelpful you are?" Neeka pouted.

"I think my room full of trophies would say otherwise," he claimed, brushing his shoulders off like he'd just been made King of the World.

"One bookshelf. You don't have a room full of trophies. Just one bookshelf, that's all."

Neeka was quiet as they pulled into the house. Her family could be so unsupportive sometimes. Why did they refuse to take her side? She was family. They should hate Annette as much as she did in that moment. She'd decided not to say anything about what Annette had said about Payton, mostly because it was the only thing the senior had said that Neeka slightly agreed with, not that she was going to follow Annette's advice. If Payton wanted extra practice, she could ask for it. Neeka wasn't going to push her into something she didn't want to do. Why couldn't people understand that? Payton wasn't her responsibility.

"How was the match, pumpkin?" her dad asked when they joined him in the den.

"It was just a practice, dad," Neeka said, giving him a hug. "If it were a match, I would have insisted you come, even if only at the end."

He kissed her on her nose. "I should have figured that out. How was practice?"

"Don't ask," Jamari and Lawanda answered in unison.

Her dad lifted an eyebrow. "That bad?"

Neeka locked her jaw, feeling her anger return. "Our captain, if you can even call her that, tried to say I wasn't working hard enough. Can you believe that? I made the varsity team all on my own, recruited by Coach Mike himself, and she has the nerve to say I'm slacking off, just like..." Neeka stopped herself.

Her mom was concerned. "It sounds like there's more to this story, something you didn't tell us in the car. Tell us everything, Neeka."

Neeka dropped onto the couch. "She said I was just like Payton."

"Is that a bad thing?" her dad asked, having only been to one of their matches. "Payton's an All Star athlete."

"It's not a bad thing if we're talking about basketball or any other sport, but volleyball—yes. I don't know, Papa, it just seems as if she doesn't care. She's always goofing around, telling those silly jokes of hers, and she never pays attention during practice. She's become a space cadet. In volleyball, where we all depend on each other, that spells trouble."

"Actually, I think trouble is spelled T-R-O-U—"

"Not now, Jamari." Lawanda cut him off.

Neeka appreciated that her mom was starting to take this seriously.

"I don't get it," Jamari said, grabbing a handful of trail mix from a bowl on the coffee table. "How can you say she's slacking off? Payton never plays. I've only seen her on the court a few times at your matches."

"Exactly," Neeka said. "Payton is a born athlete. She could be good enough at volleyball if she just put some extra effort into it. She's so used to sports coming easy to her, she refuses to work hard."

"Just because you're good at something doesn't mean you don't work hard," Jamari pointed out. "I know."

"Jamari's right," Lawanda said. "That doesn't sound like Payton."

"Bad jokes, yes. Lazy, no," her papa chimed in. "To me, it sounds like she's lacking in confidence and using humor to make up for her insecurities."

"I agree with your father," her mom said. "Payton's going through a rough time with her parents' divorce and her father moving away. He used to be her own personal coach. This is the first time she's had to go it alone. It's probably all a bit overwhelming for her. And to be honest, Neeka, I'm surprised you're not being more understanding. She's your best friend. You should know what's going on better than anyone else."

****

When dinner was finished and she was excused from the table, Neeka threw her bag into the corner of her room and pulled out her telescope. She loved looking into space. It calmed and inspired her. Around the seats of the bay window that protruded from her bedroom were an armful of astronomy books, each with hundreds of star maps.

The hobby had started when she was little. One Christmas Eve, she'd stolen her dad's binoculars and sat on an abandoned lawn chair outside in the yard to look up into the night sky in the hopes of seeing Santa and Rudolph. After a frantic search around the house, her dad had found her there, her tiny face hidden behind the massive binoculars. He scooted her over, and the two looked for Santa and his reindeer among the stars until she fell asleep in his arms.

With his long hours at work, watching the night sky was one of the few activities left that they could enjoy together. Whenever there was a huge cosmic event, like a lunar eclipse or a meteor shower, her dad would bring up two cartons of chocolate milk and they'd look through the telescope to watch the magic of the universe unfold. Those were some of her favorite moments.

One day, she'd like to float around the stars as an astronaut. Payton and she had used to joke that when they were adults, Payton would be a superstar on the WNBA while Neeka discovered super stars for NASA. They'd both be famous. In the meantime, Neeka had what seemed like millions of glow-in-the-dark stars around her room. Payton gave her a pack every year for her birthday. It was their tradition.

There was a knock on the door.

"I'm in the middle of my homework," she shouted as she quickly deserted her telescope and ran to her desk, throwing open her math book.

"Can I come in?" Jamari asked.

"Yeah, I guess," she replied coolly, still sore her family had been more concerned about Payton than her.

"Your math book is upside down," he noted as he walked in.

"I thought you were Mom."

"Good thing I wasn't."

"What do you want?" she asked impatiently.

Jamari sat on her bed, ruffling up her yellow comforter. "I haven't seen Payton around here in a good while," he commented. "You two still friends?"

"We see each other all the time. At practice. At school."

"That's never stopped you from having sleepovers before. If Payton wasn't over here, you were over at her house." He sounded troubled.

"What's your point, lizard breath? And for the record, calling it a sleepover is so last year. I'm in high school now."

"My point is—where is Payton?" He was uncharacteristically serious.

Neeka looked down. "We're both just busy with high school stuff. Geesh, we're not kids anymore. I don't play with dolls either. Surprised?"

"Payton's not a doll. She's your best friend."

"I have homework to do," Neeka insisted, hoping he'd leave. She waved her hand toward the door.

He stood but instead of walking out the room, he moved to sit on the edge of her desk. "Tell me, why do you honestly think Payton isn't doing well?"

"She goofs around in practice and doesn't attack the drills like everyone else does."

"That's what you see her doing, but that doesn't answer my question. I asked why she isn't doing well—what's causing her to goof around and freeze at practice. You ask her what's up?"

"Of course," Neeka said, defensive. "She got really angry and said she was fine then stormed away."

"Shouldn't that have been your first sign something wasn't fine? Payton is not the dramatic type. I know that as well as you do."

"So?" Neeka said, wishing the conversation were over.

"So… I can't help but wonder why you weren't more persistent. She yells at you once and you call your friendship quits? I thought you never gave up on anything. Something's not right here, Neeka."

"If you want to say something, Jamari, just spit it out, like you do all the slobber in your mouth when you're speaking. Seriously, I feel like I need an umbrella when you're sitting here talking."

Tired of her bad mood, he got up and went to the door, but stopped right before leaving. "It seems as though you're worried that, if Payton fixes her problems, she'll start playing better than you. Don't be a diva, Neeka."

He shut the door just as her math book went flying at it.

As she got up to collect it, remembering she had a quiz the next day to study for, she couldn't help but wonder if maybe he was partially right. Just maybe, she hadn't been the friend to Payton she should have been.

Shutting off her lights, she gazed around her room at all the glow-in-the-dark stars that surrounded her, each a birthday wish from Payton.

Just maybe…

CHAPTER 13

"Oh my goodness, you crack me up," Rose laughed. "Payton, you should be a comedian."

"What's so funny?" George questioned his cousin.

"Payton, tell him the joke you just told me."

Payton turned red, embarrassed. She hadn't thought Rose would actually find it funny. Most people didn't. "What did one cell say to his sister cell after she stepped on his toe?" she asked George after Rose insisted again.

"What?"

"Mitosis."

George groaned.

Yep, that's about right, Payton thought, though she didn't mind.

Rose was her new lab partner in Biology. Sometime not long after their rematch against Demonbreun High, Neeka had missed two days of school due to the flu, so Payton had partnered with Rose, whose usual partner was also sick. It seemed half the school was out that week. She and Rose had gotten along really well, so much so that they decided to stay lab partners from then on out.

"I was tired of working with a boy anyway," Rose said to her. "But he was sure cute."

Neeka didn't seem to mind. They'd been living in two separate worlds as it was. Payton felt bad, but only a little bit. It was actually refreshing to have Rose as a lab partner instead. Now, she could talk about boys and movies. With Neeka, it seemed only volleyball dominated their conversation.

Payton was happy. It was early October—officially autumn, her favorite season. The intense heat of the summer was starting to cool. It was almost bearable to walk outside again. The atmosphere around Nashville changed. People were in good form; they rode their bikes to work, headed to drive-through movies, and took long walks around the various parks of the city. One by one, the sound of air conditioners began to shut off. Her block had even organized an Elvis BBQ, where the chef dressed up like the King as he served out grilled hamburgers, hot dogs, and veggie patties.

Best of all, basketball would start up again soon. They had try-outs in a couple of weeks. Payton couldn't wait. Her heart needed that boost of confidence being good at a sport brought. Volleyball was teaching her that there was more to life than sports, and that losing wasn't the end of the world, but she still had a passion for the court. She didn't feel whole unless she was scoring points in a gym full of fans calling her name.

Dr. B called out for their attention after the morning bell rang. He took attendance then reached into his desk and pulled out several giant bags of colored marshmallows followed by packages of red licorice strings and several boxes of toothpicks.

"Sweet," Payton joked.

This time George laughed, his chair still pulled against their table. "Now that was funny." He winked.

"Don't wink at my friend, that's gross," Rose muttered.

"We've spent the week learning about the double helix structure of DNA and base pairing. Today, you'll split up into groups of four and race to build a model of DNA using the materials I supply. You'll have ten minutes. The team with the longest DNA strand wins. But it has to be accurate. You can't just throw your materials together. There are four colors of marshmallows. Each one represents a base, be it adenine, thymine, guanine, or cytosine. Remember, only certain bases can be paired together. Any models that are inaccurate will be disqualified."

"Can we eat as we work?" George asked. "I missed breakfast."

"No he didn't," Rose said. "Trust me."

"I suggest you wait until after the race is finished and has been judged. If you eat all your materials, you may not have enough to beat your competition. Feel free to choose your groups."

"I'm with you, cuz," George decided, waving his lab partner over to their table.

Payton looked apologetically toward Neeka, but she wasn't even looking at her, too involved in conversation with her new lab partner. It should have made Payton happy, but she felt an emptiness within her. This was the type of thing they would have loved doing together.

After they put their notes away and collected their materials, Dr. B gave them the signal to start. Their group raced to put together their DNA sequence. Toothpicks and marshmallows went flying, but a few found themselves into George's mouth, especially the pink ones.

"Stop eating all the cytosine," Rose objected. "We need to pair it with the guanine."

"Why?" George asked.

Rose rolled her eyes. "My goodness, you never listen in class, do you? Only cytosine and guanine can be paired together. And only adenine and thymine can be paired together. And thanks to you, we're running out."

"One minute left," Dr. B signaled.

"We have to twist it!" Payton said. "It won't count unless it's twisted like a real DNA sequence. Stop with the toothpicks and start turning it, slowly."

By the time Dr. B told them to drop what they were doing, Payton's group had a DNA model that stretched across their table. She looked around. The model Neeka's group had constructed was too short, but the group in the corner looked like they might be tough to beat. Dr. B inspected each of their sequences then returned to the front of the room.

"Group one is the winner," he announced.

Payton's group cheered.

"But ours is longer!" the group in the corner objected.

"One of your base pairs was wrong," Dr. B informed them. "You had an adenine paired with a guanine."

There was no prize for winning, but George was still smug as he ate away at their DNA model while Dr. B jumped into a lecture about how humans had over three billion base pairs in their DNA. Payton nibbled away at a string of licorice as she took notes. She hated the bitterness of normal licorice, but red licorice was delicious.

When they were dismissed to head to their next class, Dr. B stopped her to ask if she was successful in her "one step at a time" training.

"Not really. Not yet, at least," she confessed.

Yesterday had been one of her worst practices so far. Emotions were running high ever since the stunt Coach Mike had pulled with the JV team. The girls on the varsity team were afraid of making mistakes, which naturally caused them to make more. No one wanted to be viewed as a weed. Almost as if they were afraid her bad performance would spread and infect them, the other girls ignored her completely now. They even moved away when she stood next to them in line for the drills. She was almost like a ghost on the team. Even Neeka wouldn't look at her.

That was until Annette had cornered her on her way back from filling up her water bottle during a break. "You don't deserve to be here. You know why?" she asked.

Payton said nothing, partially out of fear and partially because she knew nothing would stop Annette from saying what was on her mind.

"You're not contributing. You've gotten lazy. Actually, you always have been. Why aren't you trying to get better? Don't you even care? This is a team. We're only as good as our worst player, and you are by far the worst of the worst."

Great motivational speech, Captain, Payton fumed, though she was more hurt than angry. She blinked back tears. Why did everyone assume she wasn't working hard? Was she not showing perseverance, despite all the abuse she was receiving? "I'm trying," she stammered.

"Well not hard enough. Look at Selina. At least she's showing some initiative. She's spent the entire week working with Neeka after practice. Name one time you've stayed behind to practice on your own."

It was true. Payton had never stayed late to practice, but volleyball wasn't like basketball, where a person could shoot hoops by themselves. In volleyball, she needed someone to practice with. She knew of no one on the team that would want to help her. Neeka, her closest ally, barely spoke to her these days, and she would never dare ask Lacey, who she knew was still distraught after being cut from the starting lineup, even if she refused to admit it.

It bothered Payton to know Neeka was helping Selina. How long had Neeka watched her struggle? Never once did she ever offer to help Payton. In basketball, Payton practiced with her all the time. But Neeka had been too selfish to return the favor. Payton certainly wasn't going to ask her, not after the way she'd gotten so defensive regarding volleyball these last few weeks. She'd probably take every missed serve as an insult.

"Get your act together," Annette spat before leaving.

The confrontation shook Payton. She hated any type of argument. She turned toward the locker rooms. With tears threatening to spill, she needed privacy. There was no way she was going to give the varsity team the satisfaction of seeing her cry. She could only imagine the names they'd start calling her.

"Where are you going, Moore? Practice isn't over yet." Coach Mike walked toward her with a stern frown. He was in a permanent bad mood these days. Whatever jolliness there was about him was on vacation abroad somewhere.

"I was just going to use the bathroom," she lied "I'll make it quick."

"Hold on a minute. I want to talk to you."

What now, she wondered, knowing she couldn't endure being told off a second time.

"Yeah?" she asked, her voice squeaking.

"Moore, it's no secret you haven't been playing well. Annette recruited you to be a star hitter, but you haven't lived up to our expectations. I'm sorry, kid, but you're going to have a reduced role on the team."

"Okay," she acknowledged and ran into the locker room, making it into a bathroom stall just as the tears began to spill. At least they were quiet tears. The cross-country girls who were finished for the day couldn't hear her sob. And sob she did, nonstop, using the toilet paper to wipe her nose.

She stayed in the bathroom for the rest of practice. What was the point of returning? She barely had any playing time as it was. A reduced role could only mean she was off the team. No one came looking for her, which confirmed her fears. Remembering the combination on the lock, she snuck into Neeka's locker, pulled out the cellphone hidden in the deep pocket of Neeka's backpack, and called her mom to come pick her up early.

I must convince Mom to change her mind about me not having my cellphone at school until I'm sixteen, she thought. *Then I could avoid stealing minutes from my former best friend.*

Returning the phone to Neeka's locker and making sure the metal door was shut tight, Payton had grabbed her gear and went outside to wait, allowing the autumn warmth to dry her face.

****

Payton told Dr. B the entire story, from Annette yelling at her to her mom picking her up early. He listened patiently. With her father in Cincinnati, it was nice having someone who listened to her talk, not like the way her mom only half listened when it came to sports, tears, and sweat.

"A reduced role doesn't mean you're off the team," Dr. B said. "Mike says what he means. If you were no longer on varsity, he would have said so."

"Then what does he mean? I hardly play as it is."

"I can't speak for him, Payton. But from a logical perspective, it is exactly how it sounds. You'll still be on the team, but you'll play less. That might mean you are barely on the court, but it doesn't mean you're out completely. You'll still wear the varsity jersey."

"It's hopeless," Payton sighed.

"Not necessarily. Reconsider my advice from before. Find one thing to perfect. If you're truly phenomenal at that one skill, something they can count on you to do well, then you'll very likely be called upon when they need you to do it. I don't know if you'll have time this season to figure it out, but you have an entire year to practice before next season."

"I'm already a good blocker, but that doesn't seem to matter," Payton said. "There's not a whole lot left to do."

"Find something. Something that does matter. Something no one else can do. What are you good at?"

"Nothing. Not when it comes to volleyball." Payton appreciated Dr. B's help, but she still wasn't sure exactly why he was offering it. It was apparent she was some sort of project to him, though she didn't know why.

"Then basketball. What are you good at in basketball?"

"Everything," Payton beamed.

"Why?"

"Because I can jump well, I move fast, and I always know the next move my opponents will make."

"Then start there. Use one of those skills and see if you can apply it to volleyball."

"I'll try," Payton promised.

"Don't just try. Do."

As she was about to leave, she nearly asked Dr. B if he wanted to come to one of her matches, so he could see her play and help her figure out what to do next, but she felt silly bringing the subject up, especially since she had a secret crush on him. He didn't seem like the type of teacher who enjoyed anything outside the classroom, not unless it was a science fair or something. But definitely not sports.

****

"Hey, Lacey!" Payton waved frantically, spotting Lacey in the cafeteria lunch line. Her own lunch bag in hand, she raced up to the junior. "I'm glad I found you," she said, almost out of breath. Sitting on the bench so much was having an adverse effect on her. She needed to start jogging again so that she was back in top form before basketball.

Lacey looked surprised but amused. "You okay, biscuit?" she asked.

"I just really wanted to talk to you. Can we have lunch together today?"

"Okay," Lacey said. "Just let me get my lunch first. I'm craving the butternut salad today. It looks delicious. I'll meet you at the table near Big Joe."

Payton smiled and went to the enormous inflatable cactus that towered over the cafeteria in the corner—Big Joe. Wearing red sunglasses and an absurd cowboy hat, it had been a prop for Back to the Alamo Day during spirit week, but Big Joe was so popular among the pupils, the cactus was now a permanent fixture in the cafeteria.

Soon, Lacey sat down next to her. There was no need for Payton to save a seat for her. The table was almost empty. Most of the students had elected to eat outside now that their lunch would no longer melt in the sun. Awe, autumn.

"What's on your mind, girl?" Lacey asked, taking a huge bite of her bacon burger. She must have bypassed the healthier option of the butternut salad. Payton didn't blame her. The bacon burgers at Hickory Academy were too tempting to refuse, especially when they were slathered in the school's homemade honey BBQ sauce.

Payton hesitated. She knew what she was about to ask Lacey was extremely personal, so she hoped Lacey wouldn't get upset, but Payton needed help dealing with the mess volleyball had become. That began by opening up to her teammates. Lacey was her first choice and her last option. No one but Lacey was currently talking to her.

"How do you handle not playing so much? I'm sorry to ask, but since we're in the same boat, I hope you don't mind. You seem to handle it so well."

Lacey looked as if she was about to protest, then dropped her heading, gathering the words. Finally, she looked up, smiling at the truth she was about to reveal. "I hate it. I hate it, I hate it, I hate it." She laughed. "It feels so good to say that. I understand why Neeka replaced me as setter, she's amazing, but it tears me apart sitting on the bench. I've been with the team for two years. I want to be out there, playing. I deserve to be. But I won't be. I have to accept that." She took another bite of her burger.

It was a relief for Payton to hear it. She appreciated Lacey's honesty. It had never sat well with her that Lacey had been replaced, but she knew Neeka had nothing to do with that decision. It was entirely Coach's choice. "Coach told me my role would be reduced. Seeing how little I play, I'm not sure what to make of it. I know I'm terrible, but I don't think I can stand the thought of Selina or some other new girl taking over what little playing time I had."

Lacey understood. "It was really difficult for me at first. I tried to stay positive, but I was secretly dying inside. I admit, I kind'a wanted Neeka to fail. But Neeka is outstanding. When I stopped being so angry, I actually enjoyed watching her play. And then I realized, being a sub is as important as being part of the starting lineup. We may not get the same attention, but we're the team's endurance. We have to make sure that when our sisters are growing tired, we keep the game going and win. In that way, we give our team the extra boost it needs. They count on us. More than that, they need us. No team ever won a championship match without subs. We're just as important as everyone else."

Payton could see Lacey's perspective through her eyes. She was an amazing setter. But Payton, being as bad as she was, didn't have the same skills to offer as a sub that Lacey did. Still, she felt encouraged by Lacey's optimism. She was right. Subs were just as important. She would make sure that, if she was allowed to sub in again, she'd have something fabulous to offer.

"I'm trying to come up with a special skill that I can contribute to the team, something I can transfer over from basketball, but I can't think of anything specific. Can you think of anything?" she asked.

"You're a great blocker," Lacey said.

"Yes, but blocking isn't enough. I need something more if I want to prove to Coach I'm an asset to the team, the way you are. As of now, anyone could replace me. But you and Neeka are probably the best setters in the district."

Lacey laughed. "I wouldn't say that. Why don't you go to Neeka or

Selina? I don't have a basketball background like they do."

Payton spotted Neeka across the cafeteria setting her empty tray on the vendor belt to be washed as she chatted happily with Selina. Neeka seemed to enjoy life without her. The last thing she wanted to do was ask her for help. But it was her only option.

CHAPTER 14

Cricket, Cricket, Payton thought.

Nothing eventful happened at practice that day. The girls were dead quiet, their focus solely on their drills. Coach Mike had demanded a silent practice. They were only allowed to speak when they needed to communicate their position on the court. He said it'd help them regain their focus. "Like volleyball meditation," he asserted. "And I'm your Zen master."

When practice was over, the girls continued their silence. They were allowed to talk, but they'd lost the will to, each worried about the next match they had coming up, afraid they might lose their spot on varsity if the team lost again.

Payton was the exception. She'd already hit rock bottom, so she had very little to worry about anymore. She ran up to Neeka, determined. She needed to have a chat with her former best friend, one that had nothing to do with sleepovers or Biology.

"Neeka," Payton said. "We need to talk."

Neeka looked as if she'd been expecting this. "Sure," she said, with much less resistance than Payton had assumed she'd give. She even sounded somewhat glad.

"I want you to help me. You know, the way you've been helping Selina." Her tone was full of accusation.

Neeka's face fell, but she recovered quickly. "My schedule is pretty full. I don't know if I have time."

"I don't accept that answer. I know you hate me right now for some reason, but I helped you a lot in basketball. Now you're going to help me. Right now, in fact."

Neeka looked surprised. She wasn't usually this forceful with anyone. Payton had been worried charging at her would push Neeka away, but she wasn't going to back down. Desperate times called for desperate measures. Neeka owed her.

"Fine," Neeka agreed grudgingly. "Just let me call Mom quickly to tell her I won't be on the activity bus. You'll be able to drop me off at home?"

"Yep. You can have your mom call mine if she's worried."

"Just give me a sec," Neeka said and went to the locker room to call her mom.

Five minutes later, she returned, her arms folded. Her guard was up, but Payton didn't care. This wasn't about mending their friendship. Today was all about Payton reclaiming her spot on the varsity team. Only Neeka could help her. As Lacey had pointed out, Neeka had a background in basketball. She knew Payton best. If Neeka had time to help Selina, she could help her.

"Let's head down to the middle school gym. There'll be fewer people around," Payton claimed. Truthfully, despite what she tried to tell herself, she'd be lying if she didn't hope today somehow did bring them back together. A small reason she wanted to return to the middle school was because the girls shared better memories together there than they did the high school gym. Part of Payton hoped Neeka would remember that.

They traveled down the path between the schools in silence. As they walked, Payton began to fear all this had been a mistake, that it might drive them even farther apart, if that were possible. Payton had missed Neeka a lot. She'd felt so alone on varsity. Maybe her becoming better at volleyball wasn't worth losing Neeka forever.

Neeka spoke, but only briefly. "For the record, I don't hate you, Payton. Not at all."

Payton nodded, and they continued their silence.

Walking into the middle school gym *was* like entering a time machine, just as Payton had hoped. Though Neeka had practiced here with the JV girls before being promoted to varsity, it was Payton's first time back since graduating the previous summer. But instead of being happy at the fond memories they shared playing basketball and taking PE classes here, it made Payton angry. Angrier than she had been in a long, long time.

"I can't believe how you've been treating me," she exclaimed when they reached the middle of the court. As predicted, there was no one around.

"Excuse me?" Neeka said, irritated. "I haven't done anything to you."

"That's the problem—you haven't done anything at all. You let those varsity girls get into your head. Just because they are ignoring me, you decided to as well. I thought you were better than that, Neeka, but I guess I was wrong."

"That's so not true. You're the one who stopped talking to me at practice. You were jealous." Neeka's face boiled red, though she had a touch of remorse in her voice.

"You wish," Payton snapped. She knew she had been a little bit jealous, but she wasn't going to admit it. Not if Neeka was going to deny what a bad friend she'd been. "I stopped talking because you found fault with everything I did."

"You had given up and were goofing around the whole time. What was I supposed to say, *good job*?"

"See, you're still doing it!"

"Come on, Payton. Volleyball's not coming easy to you, so what. You just need to work harder."

Who did Neeka think she was, Annette? "I have never given up, despite what everyone thinks. I've been working really hard to improve, no thanks to you. I can't believe you would help Selina but not me. That's a new low for you, Neeka."

"You never asked," she retorted. "I'm not psychic, nor am I am I responsible for you. If you wanted my help, you should have asked."

"We're best friends. At least we used to be. I shouldn't have had to ask. You saw how much I was struggling. Why didn't you offer?"

Neeka was instantly quiet, unwilling to answer. "Listen, are we here to fight or work?" she asked. "Yelling at me isn't going to make you a better volleyball player."

Still angry, Payton marched over to the equipment room and entered the security code. She knew it by heart from her days as captain of the basketball team. When the door opened, she hauled the hammock-style cart of volleyball balls out into the gym.

"We're not leaving here until I can serve, pass, and spike. You owe me that much."

****

Neeka couldn't believe how bitter Payton had become. But thinking back on Jamari's words in her room the previous night, she knew she was partially to blame. She had abandoned her friend in her time of need. Or, more accurately, she'd failed to offer the type of support a best friend was supposed to give no matter the circumstances. Unable to own up to it before, she couldn't deny that she was afraid of Payton stealing back the spotlight.

But the more Coach Mike hollered at them during practice, the more Neeka was beginning to realize the spotlight wasn't all glory. There was a lot of pressure to live up to people's expectations. The more they believed in you, the farther you fell when you let them down. Hickory Academy's three losses had showed her that.

Neeka suggested they start with the peppering drill. Serve, set, spike. It was an easy drill, covering everything Payton wanted to work on. But Payton had trouble with even the basics. Her friend clobbered around, uncoordinated. Before, when Neeka had seen Payton like this, she just assumed it was because she wasn't focusing or working as hard as she should. But now that they were one on one, Neeka witnessed firsthand both the fortitude and frustration upon Payton's face. She realized that maybe this whole time, she'd been wrong about Payton. She had spent so many years watching Payton excel at sports, it'd been hard to accept that Payton was just plain bad at volleyball.

After several more passing exercises, Neeka could identify what the problem was. It was one she herself had experienced many times in basketball. Payton was overthinking it. Because volleyball didn't come naturally to her, her mind was trying to compensate for her body.

In terms of strategy, volleyball required analysis and slow-motion thinking, but when it came to trying to force the body to move a certain way, overthinking could interfere. Like everything else in life, there was a balance that was needed. In volleyball, you had to play somewhere between your instincts and your intellect.

Neeka stopped the drill and sat Payton down on the bleachers. Her friend needed a rest. She was growing more and more frustrated. It was time they approached Payton's improvement from a different angle.

"What do you think your greatest strength is?" she asked.

Payton looked slightly embarrassed. Neeka knew she never liked talking about herself. "That's funny, Dr. B asked me the same thing earlier today."

"And what did you say?"

"My ability to jump high, move fast, and outmaneuver the competition," Payton told her. She then launched into the rest of her conversations with Dr. B, including his "master one, master all" plan.

Neeka tapped her foot, thinking. "Dr. B is right. We need to come up with a spectacular way to apply your skills to volleyball, especially your ability to jump. That's what attracted Annette to you in the first place."

"Well, it certainly hasn't helped my spike."

"I think that's because the ball is moving too fast."

Payton wasn't convinced. "That makes no sense. The ball moves just as fast in basketball."

"Yeah, but in basketball, you catch the ball. It is entirely in your control. In volleyball, you are completely reliant on those around you. The ball is only in your possession for a split second."

"So we need to think of something where I jump and have control of the ball. Great. There's nothing in volleyball like that."

Something tingled at the edge of Neeka's mind. Then she remembered what Coach Gina had taught them one day in JV practice. She lit up. "Actually, there is something exactly like that," she proclaimed excitedly.

"What?" Payton asked, intrigued.

"A topspin jump serve."

The momentary enthusiasm Payton shared with her faltered. "No one in the district can do a topspin jump serve," she protested. "Coach told us all about it. He even tried to have us practice it one day, but after Annette nearly twisted her ankle, he never brought it up again."

That was the problem with a newly formed small team. You couldn't risk any of your players, especially not your *libero*. Neeka wasn't surprised Coach Mike had left it alone. Coach Gina had never even let them try their jump serves. She'd only demonstrated them that one day.

"All the more reason to try," Neeka persisted. "I'm not saying it'll be easy, but if you learn how to do a jump serve, Coach will have to keep you on varsity. It'll mean Hickory Academy has something unique, something no other team has. Hickory Academy will have you."

Payton seemed eager again, but still not fully committed to the idea. "I just don't understand how I'll be able to get the ball over the net when I serve if I can't even do it when I jump to spike."

"It's easy. We just need to move you away from the net. The end line is about as far as you can go. It's perfect."

"Okay," Payton agreed. "I'm in. Let's do this." Feeling inspired, she jumped up, ball in hand.

They started off small, working first on Payton's approach. She squared herself off with the net then threw the ball high in the air. As soon as it left her hand, she moved forward two slow steps then two quick steps before jumping as if she was about to touch the stars. When she and the ball met, both seemingly floating in the air, she pounded the ball with the bottom of her palm before flicking her wrist.

The first ball went into the net, but Neeka wasn't worried. Everything about Payton's approach was fantastic. She just had to work on her aim when making contact with the ball. But the beauty of serving was that Payton had all the time in the world to set herself up to aim correctly. She was in complete control of the ball.

The more she smashed the ball, getting better with each jump, the more Neeka started to see the old Payton shine through. Once again, she commanded the court, her eyes set like steel in determination.

Welcome back, Neeka thought, applauding as the first ball went over the net.

****

Payton was wired after her practice with Neeka, and not just because she managed to get a few balls over the net with her jump serve. It had felt good spending time with her friend again, doing something together, just the two of them. How had they almost let their friendship go? And over something like volleyball? Up until a few months ago, neither of them had even considered the possibility they'd be on a volleyball team together.

Neeka must have felt the same because the girls agreed to go for ice cream together over the weekend. It wasn't quite a sleepover just yet, but it was better than nothing. Payton hoped that soon, they'd be back to their old selves again. Team PR.

It was late by the time her mom pulled into the driveway after dropping Neeka off at home, but the time suited her. Payton went straight upstairs to call her dad. He should be off work by now.

He picked up immediately. "This is a nice surprise, baby girl. I was just thinking about you. How is everything?"

"Good," Payton answered honestly. "I'm no better at volleyball than I used to be, but I think I'm on to something. I'm trying to master a jump serve. No one else in the district can do one, but today, I managed to do it, but it still needs a lot of work." She was talking fast, but she couldn't control herself. She was just too happy. Meeting One Direction in person type of happy. Nothing could beat getting your best friend back and finding something you were good at when it all seemed hopeless, all in the same day.

"Sounds like an excellent plan, champ. You'll knock them dead with it. They'll never see it coming."

It was a great feeling to know she could be one hundred percent truthful with her dad. Talking to him openly about the good and the bad helped her to relax a lot more than she had been earlier in the year. She didn't feel as stressed knowing her dad was still proud of her no matter how she played. He believed in her.

Now, she was starting to believe in herself again.

"You still coming down soon?"

"Not even the Titans could stop me. As soon as my schedule clears, I'm all yours."

"And what if it doesn't?"

"Then I'll call in sick. You're my main priority, baby girl."

Payton beamed. "I know you're already proud of me, Daddy, but I'm going to keep practicing the jump serve. And by the time you do make it down, you'll have a whole new reason to cheer for me."

CHAPTER 15

"I'm so hungry," Neeka said, taking a huge bit of her sandwich. "Thank goodness the flies are all gone," she added with her mouth full.

"Flies are full of protein," Dr. B said.

Was he joking? Neeka could never tell. She doubted it. He didn't seem like the type of person who told jokes. But maybe she was wrong. After their marshmallow experiment, she'd realized that though he was tough and an old fart, he wasn't as bad as his reputation made him out to be. She'd had fun that day.

She continued to eat her sandwich, letting Payton do all the talking. It was lunchtime, and Payton had insisted they spend it in the Biology lab so they could tell Dr. British about her jump serve. Apparently, he'd been giving her advice throughout the volleyball season.

Payton so has a crush on him, Neeka thought. Why else would she want to spend her lunch in this dreary lab when they could be outside?

"So at our special practice in the middle school gym, Neeka remembered Coach Gina telling the JV team no one in the district had a jump serve. Coach Mike had told varsity the same thing. But soon, I will!" she said enthusiastically.

Dr. B was pleased. "I'm glad you ladies sorted your problems out. I know you haven't been on good terms lately."

"How?" Neeka asked, tomato falling out of her mouth.

Payton elbowed her lightly in the side, warning her not to push it.

"You stopped speaking in class. Then you stopped being lab

partners. It was an easy conclusion to reach," he answered matter-of-factly, hardly any emotion behind his words.

"Yeah," Paton said, embarrassed. "I was happy Neeka was doing so well, but compared to how bad I was performing, I guess, in a way, I got intimidated. I thought it was admiration for her, and it was to some extent, but there was also a bit of jealousy mixed in. Maybe a lot of jealousy, actually."

Neeka was touched by Payton's sincerity. It gave her the courage to speak openly as well. "I loved the fact that I was better than Payton at something. I was afraid that if she started to do well, she'd steal back the spotlight. I wanted her in my shadow, for once. It was totes stupid of me to think that way."

Payton looked back at her quickly, dumfounded but not angry. Her face broke into a wide smile. Neeka wanted to get up from the table where she ate her lunch and hug her, but not in front of Dr. B. They would save their sappy ceasefire for when they were alone. He'd probably kick them out of the school if he heard them squealing.

"I missed you," Neeka mouthed silently.

"I missed you too," Payton mouthed back.

Suddenly, there was a loud, urgent knock on the door.

"Open up, it's the police," Payton joked.

Instead, a beautiful woman in her thirties walked in. She had smooth caramel skin and sleek black hair. Her eyes were amber and shone brightly. The woman reminded Neeka of a fashion model in the magazines she'd only started to read.

"I'm here for our lunch date," the woman announced.

"Excuse me for a minute, girls," Dr. B said.

She waved politely at them. "Hi, girls. I'm not interrupting a study session or anything, am I, Ron?" she asked.

"No, dear, but let's talk outside." He escorted her out of the room, apologizing for forgetting about their lunch date.

She must be Dr. B's girlfriend, Neeka guessed. They could hear her giggling on the other side of the door, so they peered through the glass, watching as Dr. B hugged her then kissed her lightly on her forehead.

Next to her, Payton frowned slightly. She was not happy. She looked confused even.

"You were crushing on him big time, weren't you?" Neeka asked gently.

Payton fumbled with a pencil on the table. "Yeah. I know he was way too old for me, but I really liked him. I know it was silly," she said, trying to hide her blush by taking a long sip of her orange juice.

"I understand," Neeka said, trying to comfort her. "I have a crush on Brad Pitt, and he's really old."

"He doesn't look it," Payton uttered.

Dr. B came back into the lab, alone, and the girls immediately dropped their heads, trying not to laugh at his lopsided glasses.

"So you're going to perfect your jump serve?" he asked, reigniting their original conversation as he fixed his glasses on top of his nose.

"Absolutely," Payton declared. "It'll give me an edge over everyone else. Even Demonbreun High doesn't have a girl who can jump serve. A few of their girls have tried during matches, but the ball always lands in the net."

"Brianna Jones on the Vikings can almost do one. She can do what is known as a float jump serve, but the one Payton is working on, the topspin jump serve, is very hard to master. But because Payton is so tall and can already jump high, she's halfway there already."

Dr. B had a blank look on his face. The terms "float" and "topspin" were another language to him. "I'm not going to pretend I know what any of that means, but it sounds like this topspin jump serve will be an asset to the team."

"Definitely," Neeka said. "According to Coach Gina, it makes the ball go high, meaning you can aim your serve almost anywhere on the court, including in the deep corners and at weak passers."

"How's your aim coming along so far? I know you said you've had trouble with it in the past when hitting."

"It needs work," Payton disclosed. "But serving is different. I have complete control of the ball. I can take my time. But it's still something I'm working on."

"We're not really sure how to fix it, not before the season ends," Neeka said.

"I suggest you record your next private practice. Then you can study the recording and see where you're going wrong. I'm sure one of those devices you kids carry around allows you to watch video in slow motion."

"That's a great idea," the girls said in unison, not sure why they hadn't thought of it before.

****

"Well done, ladies. I feel like I'm coaching varsity again," Coach Mike said as the girls circled around him at the end of practice. "You're doing much better, but still not good enough if you want to beat Demonbreun High in the District Championships. I'm doubling our next practice, so bring snacks and plenty of water. Now hit the showers."

Selina skipped up to Neeka. "Ready to help me strike them out?" she asked. "And yes, I am talking volleyball here. I want to demolish DemonRUIN High in the championships."

Oh no. Neeka had completely forgotten she was supposed to help Selina again today. Payton was also counting on her to record her in the middle school gym practicing her jump serve. Her brain spun around frantically, trying to decide the right thing to do. She finally decided Payton needed her help the most. She'd abandoned Payton for too long.

"I'm so sorry, Selina, but something has come up."

"What, you dropping me now that you and Payton are best buddies again?" Selina sneered. "I get it."

Neeka sighed. She couldn't blame Selina for being mad. "How about we meet up tomorrow after school instead? I know the cheerleaders have the gym, but we can go outside and practice. The weather's good for it. We can get milkshakes afterward to cool down."

"That's cool," Selina said. "Thanks. I'll see ya tomorrow." She did a pretend shot under the basketball hoop as she headed to the locker room, her anger gone. "Don't forget, basketball try-outs are in two weeks. Then, you'll be begging me for my help," she predicted mischievously.

"I'm a top athlete now," Neeka yelled back. "Try not to get in my way when I join the starting lineup."

Having watched Payton struggle but refuse to give up, even if it meant trading in her All Star title, Neeka had decided she would definitely still try out for basketball. She wasn't great at it, but she really did enjoy it. It would be a shame to give it up simply because it could never match her glory days on the volleyball court. She might even follow Payton's example and figure out a skill she could specialize in.

"Ready?" Payton asked. "Got your phone?"

Neeka pulled it out of her gym bag, which she'd kept out so she and Payton could hurry to the middle school gym. "Right here."

The gym was empty when they arrived, much to their relief. The JV team had already packed up and gone home, but the ball cart was left out. It sat in the middle of the gym, as if waiting for them.

Saves us a trip to the equipment room, Neeka thought, though she found it curious. Coach Gina usually never left equipment out. The net, yes, since the PE classes used it the next day. But not the balls or anything else that could easily be carried away. The doors to the gymnasium stayed opened until the security guard locked up at night. Anyone could walk in.

"I wonder why the balls were left out," Payton wondered out loud.

"I was thinking the exact same thing!" Neeka exclaimed, glad she wasn't paranoid. "Oh well. Let's count our blessings and get started."

Neeka took out her phone, and after flicking through several apps, pressed the record button as her friend practiced her jump serve, hammering the ball across the net again and again. When there was nothing left in the cart, they collected the balls then stood near the bleachers to watch the playback in slow motion.

Payton was tossing the ball too far away from her and a little too high. It was destroying her aim. Trying to aim while in the air was too late. All the work had to be done beforehand. She had to get her toss in control, and she had to align her body better with the ball upon her approach before jumping.

Emptying the ball cart a second time, Payton tried to improve her approach. They then watched the playback again to further tweak her serve, and continued the process until she nailed three jump serves in a row.

When the third serve went over the net, the girls thought they heard what sounded like a clap, but the way the gym echoed, it was impossible to know exactly where the noise came from.

"I think someone is here," Neeka hissed.

"Must be the Hickory Academy ghost," Payton said.

Neeka didn't respond, looking around.

"I was joking!" Payton laughed. "I think it came from the equipment room. Something probably just fell off a shelf. Talk about an earthquake. I pounded that last serve into the ground so hard, I bet Europe felt it."

Neeka wasn't so sure they were alone, but she shrugged it off, joining Payton in celebration over her jump serve. The more they practiced, the better Payton's timing was. Neeka giggled as, each time the serve went over the net and stayed in bounds, Payton danced on her tiptoes. Her dance looked like something out of the *Thriller* music video. By the time they finished, Payton's jump serve wasn't perfect, but it was a lot more manageable than when they first started. They left the gym arm in arm, excited for their next varsity practice when, they decided, Payton would unleash her newfound talent on the world.

What neither of the girls saw as they left was Coach Gina hiding in the bleachers, her hand over her heart, inspired by the two girls. She'd spotted them during their first private practice but said nothing. Guessing they'd be back after varsity volleyball practice, she'd left the balls out for them. She was glad she had. Witnessing what she'd just seen—the friendship and perseverance that unfolded—was a high point in her career.

CHAPTER 16

The District Championships were in a week. The JV team was finished for the year, their season over. They'd done well. With the extra experience the season had given them, a lot of the players showed promise for the varsity team next year. After JV's final match and dinner, Coach Gina had jumped courts to assist Coach Mike with the varsity team. Demonbreun High were the first seed going into the championships, but Hickory Academy was the number two seed, meaning they were ranked second for the draw. It would be a fight between the rivals to decide who left the regular season on top.

Payton grew nervous thinking about it. Excited about her jump serve, which she had practiced nonstop over the weekend, she really wanted to play against Demonbreun High. She didn't want to watch idly from the bench. Annette had put her on the team specifically to help them win the District Championship. She wanted to at least try to fulfill that role.

"Winning isn't going to be easy, so don't think I will be since we're heading toward the end of the season," Coach Mike declared. "We have one more match to win if we want to finish off the regular season in the lead. That's been our goal all year, and I'm going to push us toward it. I'm going to work you harder than I ever have before. No mercy. We'll start with the Firing Squad. Any time you miss a pass, hit, or serve, you have to do ten pushups directly in the line of fire, just like we've done in the past."

"Someone get Payton a helmet," one of the girls shouted.

Funny, Payton thought. *But we'll see who has the last laugh.*

The team was back to their good humor. They chatted keenly about the championships as they lined up. There was real hope they'd achieve their goal this year. If they won the District Championships, then all of Nashville would know they were a force to watch out for. The seniors particularly wanted to immortalize themselves on the championship plaque that would hang on the walls of Hickory Academy forever.

As usual, Payton stood at the back of the line, but this time, it wasn't because she was afraid. She wanted to prepare herself. If she screwed up her jump serve, then she would be an even bigger laughing stock than she already was. The girls would lose all respect for her, whatever little was left. Payton was tired of being the punch line of a bad volleyball joke. She wanted to be taken seriously again as an athlete.

Neeka stood just ahead of her in line. "Ready?"

"You betcha, jelly bean." Payton put her game face on.

Barely anyone noticed when her turn to serve came. She was glad. It gave her time to think, to breathe. She wanted her serve to grab their attention and never let go.

I'm in control, she said to herself.

She took her time, deciding exactly where she wanted to aim. Then she tossed the ball a fair distance into the air, moved forward, and jumped high, giving the ball her full might. She felt a power go through her, liked she'd been summoned by those above to complete this final act. It was the same feeling she always got when she was thriving at sports.

The ball went out of bounds, but the gym was stunned silent. Everyone gaped at her. Even Coach Mike needed a minute to collect his thoughts. As Payton walked over to the other side of the room to do her pushups, the whispering began.

"Did you see how high she jumped?"

"She nearly made it!"

The girl behind her in line served, but she purposely aimed for the other side of the court, avoiding Payton completely. Payton grinned as she did her pushups. Finally, a sign of respect, no matter how small. Neeka gave her a thumbs up when she returned to the back of the line. Their hard work had paid off!

When her turn to serve came again, everyone went quiet, waiting to see if her previous serve had been a fluke. Payton did the jump serve again, but this time, the ball landed in bounds. The varsity girls erupted into applause.

"So this is why you missed your practice with me last week," Selina noted to Neeka. "Well done Coach Neeka."

Payton didn't mind sharing the credit with Neeka. Her friend deserved it. Once again, they were Team PR.

Payton missed a few more serves during the drill, but a majority landed in bounds. When the team broke up to scrimmage, Coach Mike called her in to serve. She landed four aces in a row. Her serve was unstoppable. It overpowered the court. Though she left their knees sore from diving, even the girls on the other side of the net cheered her on.

From the sideline, Coach Mike pumped his fist into the air and shouted, "Yeah!"

Coach Gina squealed in delight. "Well done, Payton. I knew you could do it!"

The varsity girls had a new energy about them. More than ever, they were beginning to feel like a team again, united in a common goal instead of fighting among each other to maintain their spot on the roster. What had started as a dream at the start of the season was slowly becoming a reality. They could win the District Championships. They had a secret weapon going into their match against Demonbreun High, one their opponents could not prepare for. That gave them hope. Nothing bonded a team together more deeply than hope.

For the first time since the start of the season, Annette acknowledged Payton favorably, patting her on the back as practice ended. "You did well, girl. You're still a lousy hitter, but your jump serve makes up for it. That arm is gold. Keep it safe."

"Thanks," Payton said quietly, blushing. She was never really sure how to handle Annette. The girl lived in total opposites, either full of praise or full of criticism.

Coach Gina came up to her next. "You see that," she said, indicating the confident smiles and animated chatter of the girls around her. "You did that. You never gave up, Payton. And because of that, neither will this team." She hugged her then directed her toward Coach Mike. "The big guy wants to talk to you."

Coach Mike was staring down at his clipboard when Payton joined him at the far side of the gym. It looked like he was making notes to the roster. He ran a hand threw his spiky blonde hair then scribbled with his pen. Ink stained his fingertips.

"You surprised us today, Moore," he said without looking up. "How long have you been working on that secret weapon of yours?"

"Not long," Payton conceded.

"No matter." He looked up at her. "I hope you're ready for battle. I'll be calling you in to serve during the championships."

****

With the district, regional, and state tournaments ahead of them—all post-season events—the regular season District Championships weren't as glamorous as the tournaments to come, but it was still very important, especially to Hickory Academy. They had fought all year to get this far. They weren't going to back down now. True, they'd be competing in the post-season district tournament, but knowing they'd lost to the Hawks and lesser teams before, the seniors were aware this match could be the last shot they had at winning a championship title. They had secured their place in the final here. That was the only thing that was certain. Tournaments could go either way. They weren't as experienced as some of the other teams. In sports, experience was everything. So it was either now or never if they wanted to bring home a trophy.

And we want it bad, Payton thought, looking at the girls around her as they gathered for a huddle before their match against Demonbreun High began. They were in the Cougars' gym, neutral territory since the

Cougars were out for the season. They'd put in a good fight though, being their first year. The stands were packed as teams and fans from all over sat down to watch the final match of the regular season.

Payton's dad couldn't make it down for the match. It annoyed her. He'd promised to put her first, but he'd insisted that he'd come down for the entire district tournament. It was a fair compromise, but if this was Hickory Academy's one shot at championship glory, she wished he'd chosen this match to attend.

"This is it, girls," Annette said, a fierce determination in her eyes. She'd sell her own kidney to win. Moreover, she'd expect the rest of the team to do the same. "All or nothing. Don't let me down."

"Great speech, as always," Neeka whispered sarcastically to Payton. "Talk about using fear as a motivational technique. Only problem is, it doesn't work."

"Then do better," Payton encouraged her. "You're a leader on this team, Neeka, whether you want that responsibility or not, though I think you do. You have as much right to step in there and say something to the girls as Annette does."

"Not really," Neeka said uncertainly. "Annette is captain."

"She won't be next year. Someone needs to fill her spot. This could potentially be our last match of the season. Show Coach Mike that you're the best choice."

Payton had never *not* been captain of a sports team, but she knew Neeka would be outstanding at it when it came to volleyball, much better than her. Neeka had the skills and the stamina. She could see the full picture of what was happening around her, and she was very, very patient, something Payton had seen firsthand while working on her jump serve. Granted, Neeka had misread Payton's behavior at practice, but the season had been a learning experience for them both.

Neeka was indecisive. "I don't know. There's an etiquette to these things, rules of conduct that would be rude to ignore. It wouldn't be very sportsmanlike."

"This is Annette we're talking about. I don't think she knows what etiquette is. You'd better hurry. Coach Mike is on his way. Once he starts giving his speech, your opportunity is lost."

Payton shoved her slightly forward, but Neeka hesitated.

"Payton…"

"Girls, I hope you brought your warrior spirits with you," Coach Mike began. "This is what we've been waiting for."

It was too late. Neeka rejoined Payton by her side, meeting Payton's glance with a shrug. "Next time," she mouthed.

But they both knew there might not be a next time. Not at a final match for a championship title. At least, not this season.

Coach Mike continued his pep talk, which was pretty much a summary of how far the girls had come over the last three years since the volleyball program had their inaugural match. He told them he was proud of them, but that they were fighters and need to keep battling until the end. Some of the seniors had tears in their eyes, sad that it was their last regular season match but pleased they had proven themselves worthy competitors within the district over the last three years.

They wiped their tears away as they took their positions on the court. Hickory Academy won the coin toss and chose to serve, but Payton remained on the bench. They didn't want to reveal her jump serve just yet. She would be their surprise attack.

The match began. This was it! Next to her, Lacey squeezed her hand nervously as the first serve was made. Selina cheered. The other subs stomped their feet. It was mayhem on the sidelines.

The Demonbreun High players were as focused as ever. There was a reason they were the top seed. But they'd lost to the Vikings and another team, so they would have to work hard if they wanted to defend their championship title, especially now that Payton had discovered her jump serve. Nothing was guaranteed. That was the beauty of sports. In all the years Payton had watched sports on TV with her father, she had often seen underdogs go on to become heroes, fueled solely on the cheers of their fans. Miracles happened under stadium lights.

Not that Hickory Academy needed a miracle to win. They were skilled, there was no denying that. Neeka and Annette especially. Their faces glistened with sweat and their eyes were intense with concentration as they went to war with Demonbreun High, already masters of the court.

For what felt like hours, Payton watched as the ball flew between the two sides of the net. There was rally after endless rally. And then, her turn came.

"Tornado, you're up," Coach Mike shouted, subbing her in.

"Good luck," Lacey said.

Nervous but full of anticipation, Payton took her position behind the end line. The Demonbreun High girls were confused. She could hear it in the way they shouted at each other, unsure of what positions to take. Her serves usually went straight into the net. Why would Hickory Academy sub in their worst player so early in the match? In the end, they moved forward toward the net, where they expected the ball to go, leaving the deep corners unprotected.

Perfect, Payton thought then focused. Taking a deep breath to steady herself, she prepared her body and mind. Blocking out all distractions, she tossed the ball and, moving instinctively, jumped high before slamming it hard so that it reached the back of the court. She was relieved when it stayed in bounds, her aim still a little shy at times.

Fans on both sides gasped. That was not what they had expected to see. Then the Hickory Academy crowd broke out into crazy cheers, which they repeated every time Payton served the ball. Her reign only ended when the Demonbreun High *libero* was finally able to dig the ball. The girls in black and yellow won the rally and prepared to serve.

The rest of the match was a close fight. Up until the very end, no one was really sure who would win. By the fourth set of the match, knowing Payton was only subbed in to serve, the fans started yelling, "One Moore Minute! One Moore Minute!" every time she retook her place on the bench after giving Demonbreun High a run for their money.

Bones were nearly broken during the fifth set as the girls dived for the ball. The starting lineup grew tired fast, and the subs were brought in frequently to allow them a quick break to recover from their bruises. At one point, Selina did a pancake dive, fanning her hand out flat to stop the ball from touching the floor. It was a legal move, but they were only allowed to use it in extreme emergencies because it came with the risk of injury, since the person diving had to literally fall flat on floor. Sure enough, with no time to properly dive, Selina banged her chin hard against the wood.

"At least I saved the ball," she said, a little dazed as she stood and went into her ready position.

"That you did," Payton heard Lacey say back.

Hickory Academy played an amazing set, but it wasn't enough. Demonbreun High gripped their lead all the way to the final buzzer. As the regular season closed out, it was Demonbreun High who walked away as District Champions for yet another year in a row. Hickory Academy was second.

****

The following Monday at school, there was no sign that Hickory Academy had lost. After watching their performance at the District Championships, a fever for victory spread. The student body's hopes were high regarding the post-season. Varsity volleyball had grabbed their attention and earned their respect.

As Payton walked through the corridors, she was astonished to see the hundreds of Vs their classmates had cut out of blue paper and hung around the school, each with well wishes written on the side. People she'd never met before patted her on the back, even the principal. Being on the volleyball team had made all of the varsity girls famous at the school.

Neeka came running up to her. "Oh my God, Payton, you have to see this," she said, pulling on her arm.

Payton giggled. "Slow down, Neeka. We'll get in trouble for running."

"Who cares!" Neeka shouted, leading the way. "You won't after you see this."

She guided Payton into the grand hallway. Payton looked around, but besides the numerous Vs taped to the side of the lockers, she didn't notice anything special. "What?" she asked.

"Look up," Neeka said, pointing to the ceiling.

Payton's heart nearly stopped when she saw the banner that was strewn across the grand hallway. High above her head, her name was written in silver glitter. She swallowed to hold back her tears, her emotions running high.

So this is what happens when you refuse to give up at something that doesn't come naturally. It may take a long time, but eventually, you find your own personal victory, she thought. Because she'd had to work so hard at volleyball, the words on the banner meant more to her than any trophy she'd ever earned as an All Star.

One Moore Minute.

CHAPTER 17

This. Was. Totally. Massive.

Any expectations Payton had for the Regional Final flew out the window the moment she stepped into the enormous gymnasium of the university hosting the match. The ceiling was so high, a plane could fly through. The bleachers, though that was an understatement to call them that since some of the sections had actual cushioned seats, were filled with not only fans, but a full news crew from the state sports channel. The cameras were pointed at them, Hickory Academy. And the team they were playing—the Centurions.

A woman with a notepad poked her in the side. "Payton Moore, Carrie Brooklyn from the Nashville Independent. How does it feel being a diamond in the rough? Your stats earlier this season were, shall we say... quite poor. And now you've surprised the high school volleyball community in Tennessee with your amazing jump serve. How do you explain your unexpected comeback?"

I wouldn't call it a comeback, Payton thought. *I'm still only mediocre at everything else, except blocking, but my strikes are so bad, Coach won't even let me near the front row.*

She opened her mouth to answer but was interrupted by Coach Gina. "Carrie, you know better than to bother my girls before a big match. You can interview them afterwards," she said, rounding the varsity team up.

Payton thanked her. "I wasn't sure how to comment."

"Well, there's no need to comment until the final is over. Carrie knows that. Don't mind the media; just keep your head in the game. As far as you're concerned, no one else exists except your team."

She tried to focus, but Payton couldn't help but be in awe by everything around her. The bright lights. The fans dressed in blue wigs. The massive trophy sitting on the presentation table near the back wall. Coach Mike wearing a suit! Well, kind of. He had on slacks and a crisp blue polo shirt. His suit jacket was flung across the bench, hardly worn. Payton wondered if this is what the gladiators felt like standing in the middle of the Roman Coliseum. It was equally terrifying and fascinating.

If this is the Coliseum, then we're the lions about to attack, Payton told herself for motivation.

It'd been a short journey to the Regional Final. A lot shorter than she would have thought after losing the regular season District Championships to Demonbreun High. Hickory Academy never imagined that they'd be here. Yet here they were, battling for a chance to advance to the Sub-State match and then, if they played their cards right, to State itself.

"You okay?" Neeka asked her.

"More than okay. I feel like I won a ticket to the Teen Choice Awards. I mean, I know I've played big championships before, but never at a high school level. This is a first. Everything is just so…"

"Big?" Neeka finished the sentence for her.

"Exactly."

And to think, Payton thought to herself. *This was all because of a lucky doorknob…*

****

A week before, the Hickory Academy varsity volleyball team had been preparing for the post-season District Tournament. Their hopes of winning weren't high, but they were glad that they weren't hanging up their jerseys just yet, especially the seniors. The tournament consisted of two days of game play at various high schools throughout the district. They'd be matched against the same teams as during the regular season, but this particular tournament decided who went on to the Regional Tournament. All the highest ranked teams in the district were playing, including Demonbreun High, who were the favorites to win, and the Vikings. It'd be intense.

"Hey, did any of you hear the story of the lucky doorknob?" Selina asked as the girls stretched out before practice. "I just heard about it today."

The older teammates moaned.

"That's just something the teachers tell freshies like yourself to keep them from freaking out during high school. If a student has a panic attack before a test, they're told to touch the lucky doorknob. If someone cries because they got detention for the first time for being late to class, they're told to touch the lucky doorknob. You get it," Annette explained. "We don't have time for children's stories, Selina. We have a tournament to focus on."

"But isn't it worth a try, just in case it might help?" Selina persisted.

Annette gave her one of her icy stares and Selina immediately dropped the subject, but Payton and Neeka were intrigued. They wanted to know more, so they called Selina over to them when the girls lined up for their first drills of the practice.

"What's the story of the lucky doorknob?" Payton asked, loving a good mystery.

"In the library, there's a doorknob made out of stained glass in all different colors, but mostly blues and greens, since it was made by a Hickory Academy student. It's kind of triangular and abstract, like that painter with all the funny faces and shapes, Tabasco."

"Picasso," Neeka corrected her.

"Who cares. Anyway, it's right behind all the old atlases in the library, attached to the wall. It's on display; anyone can touch it. The legend goes that years ago, back in the olden days before the new extension was built, the art room was located in the basement. One day, a fire broke out in the one of the pottery kilns. Being the basement, the windows were too high up to climb to and too small to crawl through, even if the students could reach them, so everyone in the room went running for the door, but it was stuck. The heat from the fire had melted the doorknob from the inside. The students and the art teacher were stuck, with nowhere to go."

"Is this a true story?" Payton asked, skeptical.

"Let me finish," Selina insisted. "Then you can decide, but it sounds pretty legit to me. Anyway, one of the students was in the middle of making a round glass sculpture. He hadn't intended for it to be a doorknob, but he realized it was the perfect size. Taking his art chisel, he tore the melted doorknob off and replaced it with his sculpture. He used it to open the door, freeing everyone trapped just as the flames from the kiln engulfed the room."

"What does that have to do with luck?" Neeka asked. "It sounds more like resourcefulness."

"Well, it was lucky he even had the sculpture on him. You can be as resourceful as you want, but if you don't have the necessary tools, you don't escape," Selina pointed out.

It was a good point. Payton was fascinated, throwing her suspicions as to whether or not the story was true aside. It made a good tale. "So why is it hanging on the library wall?"

"According to Mrs. Turtle—"

"Wait, Mrs. Turtle told you this story?" Neeka asked. "Now I'm slightly impressed. She's about the most boring person in the school, even worse than Dr. B. There's no way she'd come up with this on her own."

"Of course she didn't. This is a Hickory Academy legend. It's been passed down through the generations. I bet Payton's dad has even heard of it."

"Maybe he was the one who made the sculpture!" Neeka speculated jokingly.

"No way. The only thing my dad can make is paper planes."

"ANYWAY," Selina said, wanting to finish the story, "after the firefighters put out the flames, the only thing left among the ashes was the glass doorknob. As a tribute to the art student that had saved the day, they hung it up in the library, vowing to keep it there as long as the school stood. Since that day, there has never been another fire at

Hickory Academy, not even a small one. As the years passed, teachers and staff started thinking it was because of the doorknob, as if it had magical properties that protected the school. For fun, one year, the entire football team touched the doorknob for luck. That year, they won state. Mrs. Turtle said that, in the past, every team in the school used to touch the lucky doorknob before the start of the season, after hearing about the state win for the football team. But she says that as the years have gone by, belief in the lucky doorknob isn't as popular as it used to be."

"Wow," Payton said, flabbergasted. "That is some story."

"Why are we only hearing about this now?" Neeka wondered.

"You heard Annette's reaction," Payton said. "They must not believe in it."

"But we do?" Selina asked, searching for confirmation from the girls.

"Of course!" they both said.

Selina smiled like a mad scientist about to take over the world. "Then it's obvious what we need to do…"

"We need to convince the rest of the varsity team to touch the lucky doorknob," Neeka said. "But how?"

"We'll trick them if we have to," Selina suggested.

Payton shook her head. "No, it might backfire. I have a feeling everyone has to touch it of their own free will for it to work. We'll have to convince them to, when the time is right."

With the District Tournament less than a day away, they knew it would have to be soon. They were able to recruit a few girls by the end of practice, but try as they might, most of the girls refused, calling it a silly tradition. It looked like the lucky doorknob would have to wait for another team to avail of its charm.

****

The next morning, Payton woke with the sunrise. Her alarm

wouldn't go off for a few more hours, but she was too anxious to sleep. It was the first day of the District Tournament and very likely the second to last day of the volleyball season. They were confident they would make it to the finals the next day, but they were certain any number of teams could beat them there, particularly Demonbreun High. They were 1-2 when it came to their rivals, who were way more experienced at championship matches then they were.

Payton was glad to be moving on to basketball. Try-outs had been the previous week. She hadn't made varsity, but in basketball, that was near impossible as a freshman. Barely any sophomores were even upgraded. On the bright side, she was JV Captain. Also, Neeka had made it onto the roster. Though Neeka was only a sub, Payton gave her the same speech Lacey had given her under Big Joe, the cactus in the cafeteria. No team won a championship without subs. That was as true for basketball as it was volleyball.

She couldn't wait for basketball to begin, but leaving volleyball was bittersweet, especially now that her jump serve was getting closer and closer to being mastered. Her aim had improved so much from the first time she and Neeka had practiced it. She had never thought she'd say this at the start of the volleyball season, when she could barely pass the ball, but she was looking forward to volleyball season her sophomore year, determined to continue practicing so she returned a more skilled player all round.

Yawning, she rolled out of her Titan comforter and onto the floor, her body still trying to catch up with her mind. Her cell phone rang just as she was about to go downstairs and make herself a cup of hot chocolate, as was her Saturday ritual.

"Hello?" she answered groggily, wondering who was calling so early. She was afraid the phone had woken her mother, who was still sound asleep.

"Payton, it's Neeka. You won't believe this, but I just got a text from Annette. Lacey jammed her fingers into her car door last night and can't play today. There's a possibility she might play tomorrow, if the swelling goes down, but she's definitely out today."

"What are we going to do?" Payton panicked. "She's your sub."

"Coach has already called in the JV setter that replaced me. That sophomore girl from Memphis. So no worries there. But this isn't a good start to the post-season. That's why I'm rallying the troops. Come downstairs. We're parked outside."

What? Payton wasn't sure what was happening. "I'm in my pajamas," she protested.

"Don't worry, we all are," Neeka said. "Just come down. Try not to wake your mom."

The sun was barely up and already they were on a covert mission. Payton tiptoed downstairs and quietly opened the front door. Outside, Jamari's jeep was parked in her driveway. The entire varsity team was packed inside, each in their pajamas, just as Neeka had promised.

She closed the front door quietly then raced to the jeep. Neeka had saved her a spot in the front next to her. "What is all this about?" she asked, buckling her seatbelt.

"The lucky doorknob," the entire jeep sang.

"I'm loving this!" Jamari laughed. "That doorknob must be lucky if it means I get to drive a jeep full of pretty volleyball girls around in their pajamas."

"Hey, eyes on the road," Neeka said. "No gawking at my team."

As she gazed around the jeep, she was surprised to see Annette in the very back, along with Lacey. Gauze tape covered Lacey's hand. *Ouch.* But more surprising than seeing Lacey's injured fingers was the smile on Annette's face. Dressed in a purple onesie, she was actually enjoying this.

They made one last stop to pick up Janette, the sophomore taking Lacey's place on the team for the day. "Might as well be thorough," Neeka had said outside her door. Janette was a quiet girl with mousy brown hair and wide doll eyes. She crammed herself into the jeep wearing Titans boxer shorts with a long sleeve t-shirt. Payton liked her immediately.

"Why do I have to touch the doorknob?" Lacey asked, wriggling her feet around in her bunny slippers. "I'm not playing today. I'm injured. I need my beauty sleep."

"Girl, you look like you've gotten plenty of beauty sleep to me," Jamari said.

Neeka flicked him across the forehead as Annette said, "You being injured is exactly why you need to touch the lucky doorknob. In fact, I think you should be the first to do so."

When they got to the school, they met the first challenge of their quest. The doors were locked. The lights were out. No one was home.

"How did we not predict this?" Annette whined.

"We did," Neeka said. "I've recruited a secret agent."

As she spoke, a black convertible pulled into the parking lot. Looking freshly pampered and wearing designer jeans and a Hickory Academy volleyball hoodie, Coach Gina stepped out. "Hi, girls," she said brightly. "And boy," she greeted Jamari.

She must have already drunk a gallon of coffee to be so chirpy this early, Payton thought, thinking of her mom who was probably still snoring away with curlers in her hair.

From her pocket, Coach Gina pulled out a key and shook it in the air. "Ready?"

The gang followed her into the school. It was an in and out mission, so there was no need to turn on all the lights. Instead, they huddled together in the near darkness, the sun not quite high enough in the sky to light up the corridors. Bumping into each other as they walked, even though most had their phones out to add extra light, they finally made it to the library. Coach Gina flicked on the lights.

"That better not have been you touching my arm," Annette barked at Jamari.

"Hey, I'm a gentleman. I kept my distance," he insisted. "Plus, I'm more into Latina girls," he said, looking over at Lacey.

"In your dreams," she said, laughing.

Selina marched them down toward the atlases. As they rounded a large bookshelf, they came upon the doorknob for the first time. It was just as Selina described. Made of stained glass in various shades of blue, green, purple, and yellow, it sparkled in the bright sunlight that had started to stream through the windows. It was attached to a white marble plaque that read, "Even the most unassuming wonders guard these walls."

"Who's first?" Coach Gina asked.

"Lacey!" the team shouted.

Rolling her eyes but giggling, Lacey reached forward and touched the lucky doorknob with her injured hand. She was followed by everyone else on the team, including Coach Gina. The surface was smooth against Payton's hand. She didn't feel any different, but it was exciting nonetheless.

"Wait a minute," Jamari said, the last to touch it. He represented their fans. "If everyone on the team has to touch it, what about Coach Mike?"

"You, don't worry about him. Mike is one of the most superstitious people I know. He would hang the doorknob in his office if they let him. He touches it nearly every morning," Coach Gina informed them. "It's a daily ritual to him."

"Now we know how Payton suddenly learned how to do a jump serve," Selina joked, but no one laughed.

Their hopes running high, Jamari drove all of the girls back home to change out of their pajamas and prepare for the District Tournament. It would be a long day with three different matches to play. The brother and sister duo dropped Payton off last.

"See you later, jelly bean," Payton said, closing the door.

"Let's show them what Team PR can do!" Neeka shouted out the window as Jamari drove away.

Payton was never so glad to have her friend back. She'd missed her more than she'd realized these last two months. And Jamari too. But now Neeka and she were ready to face high school the way they were meant to—standing together side by side.

****

Maybe it was the doorknob. Maybe it was written in the stars. Or maybe it was just a result of a crazy, chaotic world. Hickory Academy did make it to the District Tournament Final the following day, but they weren't up against Demonbreun High. In an unexpected turn of events, Demonbreun High lost in the semi-finals against the Vikings.

It's almost poetic, Payton thought. The two best servers in the district,

Brianna Jones and her, would face off in the battle that would determine who moved on to the Regional Tournament. It was the horned helmets versus the blue wigs—a fight no one had predicted.

Payton hated to say it, but it was an easy match to win. Brianna Jones was no doubt the best player on the Vikings, but her talent wasn't enough to hold up the team. The Vikings were clearly still exhausted from their match against Demonbreun High. That was the problem with fighting to the death. It sometimes meant there was no life leftover for the next match. Hickory Academy won by a large lead. And with their victory, they advanced to the Regional Tournament.

"Unbelievable." Lacey sighed, standing beside her as they accepted their trophy. "This is more than any of us dreamed of last year." Her hand was still bandaged, but with the swelling down, the injury wasn't as bad as everyone had originally feared. Coach Mike had let her play a few minutes in the final, when their win was nearly guaranteed, so she wasn't left out.

"I know," Payton said. "I can't believe it."

"Thank goodness for lucky doorknobs," the junior mused, rubbing her hand gratefully.

****

"Earth to Payton," Neeka said, waving a hand in front of Payton's face. She shook her head, leaving behind her memories of the past week and focusing on the Regional Tournament Final at hand. It'd been a tense battle to the final. They'd nearly been knocked out during the quarter finals and semi-finals the previous day. The teams they'd played were unfamiliar. They didn't know what to expect. But the opposite was also true. No one knew much about Hickory Academy. They were novices to the Regional Tournament arena, the new girls, and wrongly underestimated.

Upon the signal from the referee, the girls ran out onto the court and stood in formation as the loudspeakers called out each of their names. The Centurions stood in front of them. As the fans cheered with each name the announcer yelled out, the two teams sized each other up. The Centurions had made it to the Regional Tournament the year before, but they'd lost in the quarter final. This was their first trip to the championship match. They didn't look intimidating or aggressive; they just appeared to be a group of girls who were just as excited to be there as Hickory Academy.

Adjusting her kneepads, Payton looked into the bleachers where her dad sat next to her mom and the Leigh family, including Donald. Her dad had missed the District Tournament, breaking his promise, but to make up for it, he'd taken the whole next week off work. So though he had made it down just in time for the final of the Regional Tournament, checking into a hotel somewhere within Mt. Juliet, where the matches were being held, he'd spend the next five days with her in Nashville. That was enough for her.

The referee blew his whistle again, and the girls ran to quickly slap the hands of the Centurions before huddling together for a quick pep talk from Annette. Then Payton, Selina, Lacey, and the other subs headed to the bench while the starting lineup took their positions on the court. They bounced around, keeping warm before service began. Before long, the match was underway.

For the first time all season, Payton cheered along with the other subs, putting aside her jealousy. Again, she looked up into the bleachers at her dad as she shouted and clapped. She couldn't wait to get into the game. She wanted so bad to show him what she could do. Above his head, he held a sign that read, "Moore to Win!" He shook it when he saw her looking up and smiled.

Hickory Academy lost the first set, but they won the next two. As they entered the fourth set, Payton looked anxiously at Coach Mike. She was usually subbed in by now to unleash her jump serve. Selina and Lacey had been in and out a few times. Why hadn't he used her yet?

Sensing her stare his way, he turned to her and said, "Psychological warfare. I'm waiting for the Centurions to get comfortable. Then we'll blast them."

Better make that soon. The match is almost over, she sulked, looking at her dad yet again.

Just as Hickory Academy took a six-point lead, Coach Mike finally called her in. As she walked toward the court, ready to send the Centurions back to ancient Rome, Coach Mike grabbed her jersey, pulling her aside. "Killer instinct. Close it out."

"Nothing less," she promised, and she did just that. Jumping in the air like a panther after its prey, Payton brought her team to the winning score. The local headlines the next morning would broadcast to the world that Hickory Academy were champions of their Regional Tournament.

****

"And the MVP of the match goes too…" the announcer paused for dramatic effect.

Payton squeezed Neeka's arm. "You so have this," she said to her friend. Neeka deserved it. Because of her flawless setting, the hitters were able to do serious damage with the ball. Moreover, she'd been a leader on the court, shouting encouragement out to her fellow teammates.

They were lined up on the podium, waiting for their trophy to be delivered. First, the announcer had to go through the formalities of thanking the officials, coaches, and sponsors. And revealing who had been voted MVP—Most Valuable Player.

"Annette Reynolds, the captain and *libero* for Hickory Academy," he announced over the loudspeaker.

Neeka's face dropped, but she applauded with the rest of the team. Payton thought it was unfair. Neeka deserved the MVP trophy, not Annette. She'd been more of a leader than the senior. The girls on the team respected her instead of feared her. Plus, she'd played like a pro, even with the pressure of the media watching.

"Don't feel bad for me. She's a senior, let her have her moment," Neeka said, reading Payton's thoughts. Maybe they did have a psychic connection like twins.

The moment to accept their trophy came. As the officials prepared to formally declare Hickory Academy as Regional Champions, the girls on the team suddenly became nervous, unsure of how they were supposed to respond upon accepting their trophy. Did they jump up and down? Or were they meant to be more serious?

In the end, they blushed appreciatively, waiting until after the team photo was taken before breaking out into more jubilant screams and cheers. Selina punched her arm straight into the air, causing the Hickory Academy fans to roar. A good majority of the student body had driven out to watch them play, and they had been rewarded for their efforts.

One thing was for certain, Hickory Academy had acquired a fine taste for victory. They'd exceeded even their expectations. And now that they were here, they wouldn't settle for anything less than the State Championship. But first, they had to win their Sub-State match.

CHAPTER 18

The gymnasium selected for their Sub-State match wasn't as titanic as the one they played in during the Regional Tournament Final. It didn't have cushioned seats or abnormally high ceilings. There was no press box the media could comfortably fit into. In fact, the bleachers that surrounded the gym floor were quite old and rickety. But Hickory Academy did not care. It was their venue of choice, because it was their own gymnasium. They'd won home court advantage for the single match that would decide who went to State.

As a result, they were surrounded by cascading blue and green waterfalls. The cheerleaders and spirit committee had spent hours decorating the gym in glittering streamers that flowed like water down the aisles of the bleachers. Among the streamers sat almost everyone from the school, including Dr. B. The gymnasium had never had so many people within its walls before. It was the first time in recent memory that Hickory Academy had a full house.

More than a full house, Neeka fretted, hoping the bleachers didn't give way. The scene reminded her of an old carnival ride about to break down. She swore she even saw them sway back and forth, but that could have been the football team and their antics.

For the Sub-State Tournament, Hickory Academy had been paired with Gold Bay. Neeka had thought it was a funny name for a school, since the entire state of North Carolina sat between Tennessee and the

Atlantic Ocean. Around the state, nearly a dozen teams were battling against each other, the winner of each heading to the State Tournament. There was only one match to play, and one match to win, before the crusade for the State trophy truly began.

Gold Bay hadn't travelled too far to challenge Hickory Academy in Nashville, so they'd brought a lot of their fans with them. Among familiar faces and unfamiliar faces alike, a restlessness ran through the crowd. The excitement of advancing had been replaced by pure nerves, both from the fans and players.

"Does everyone seem on edge to you?" Neeka asked Lacey as they warmed up together, setting the ball high in the air.

"It's like we've all been infected with a massive case of the jitter bugs," Lacey observed, agreeing with Neeka that the energy in the gymnasium was different than that of the matches before. "I guess that's what happens when you get this far up. People stop being surprised you win and start expecting it."

"Well, I have no idea what to expect," Neeka mumbled. "Are we really prepared for this?" Until they'd learned who they were paired up against, she had never even heard of Gold Bay. No one on the team had, not even Coach Mike. They'd never needed to, this being the first time the Hickory Academy volleyball program had advanced away from their district.

The whistle for the players to lineup blew.

"I guess we're about to find out," Lacey said, running over to join the team on the court for the pre-match announcements.

Neeka barely paid attention to the opening ceremonies, her mind already in the game. Gold Bay had strong, durable players. They weren't super tall, not like Payton or the Demonbreun High girls, but they were taller than most of the Hickory Academy team, and they were built, looking more like women wrestlers than volleyball players. That meant they'd pack a powerful kill shot. Hickory Academy would have to take the defense, aiming their strikes toward the back of the court to keep the Gold Bay passers off guard, Neeka noted, forming a list of strategies to discuss with Coach Mike and the rest of the team.

As the match began and the first set was played, Neeka's predictions proved correct. Gold Bay had some pretty mighty hitters. Annette and the back row took a beating as they dived for the balls that reached them, but a majority of kill shots made by Gold Bay were aimed close to the net, putting pressure on Hickory Academy's front row to block and pass. It was a good strategy, one the home team was not prepared for. As Neeka set the ball, she could tell the hitters she was setting for were growing tired quickly. To compensate, she called out to the back row to strike from behind the ten-foot line more often than normal. It was as though they were playing the game in reverse.

We have to get control of the situation, Neeka thought, knowing they couldn't continue on like this.

The first two sets went to Gold Bay. During a time-out halfway through the third set, Coach Mike sat the girls down to review their strategy. Gold Bay was leading. Hickory Academy was minutes away from losing the match and all their hopes at competing in the State Tournaments. They had to do something, and they had to do it fast.

Suddenly, a chant started in the bleachers.

"One Moore Minute! One Moore Minute! One Moore Minute!"

The home team fans were calling for Payton to play.

"Coach?" she questioned, ready to serve.

"Not yet," Coach Mike decided. "Not until they least expect it. It worked for Regionals. It'll work here too. Besides, your serve isn't enough to save this match. Think," he said firmly to himself, tapping the clipboard against his head. Their time was running out. They'd be called back to the court soon.

"Switch it up," Coach Gina suggested. "Put the hitters in the back row and move your passers to the front."

Coach Mike considered this. "That just might work," he said excitedly. "Gina, I'd kiss you if my wife wasn't two feet away. You're a genius!"

The assistant coach waved his compliment away. "It was logical," she claimed modestly. "Let's just hope it works."

"What are you waiting for?" Coach Mike yelled at them. "Get back on to the court! You know the plan."

When the serve came over their net, they quickly changed into their new formations. For whatever bizarre reason, the strategy worked. Hickory Academy galloped back into the running, winning the third and fourth sets. They weren't going to let the State trophy slip out of their hands so easily.

"I can feel your hunger!" Coach Mike yelled from the sidelines. "Devour them!"

Up 11-8 in the final set, Hickory Academy had victory by the edge of their teeth, but the rallies had been well coordinated on both sides of the net, especially since the third set. It was anyone's game. Neeka refused to lose focus. Her mind wanted to speed up to the end of the match, but she forced it to move in slow motion so that she could set properly. She didn't want to get sloppy, not like she had those three losses toward the end of the regular season.

Gold Bay won back the serve and managed to score a second point before Hickory Academy got the side-out. With only three points left to win the match and Gold Bay catching up fast, the team rotated, but before her teammate in the far right of the back row had a chance to even pick up the ball to serve, Neeka heard the crowd go wild.

"One Moore Minute!" they shouted.

Coach had finally sent Payton in to sub. He wanted her to take home the final points of the match. Almost relieved, the hitter she was replacing ran to the bench, allowing Payton to prepare for the jump serve. Her first serve landed in the back of the court, just as the Gold Bay *libero* dived for it.

Point.

Then, to the surprise of even Coach Mike, Payton changed from a topspin jump serve to a floating jump serve. Unprepared for the lower, tighter serve, the hitter closest to the ball passed it awkwardly to no one in particular. The ball went out of bounds and the hitter went flying to the floor.

Point.

Neeka braced herself in her ready position, confident Payton could close out the set. The Gold Bay girls were falling all over the place. Hickory Academy was about to triumph.

State, here we come! Neeka yelped inwardly, dancing inside.

But Payton's third serve wasn't as sharp. The *libero* on the opposite side of the court was able to dig it, and when Annette failed to reach a spiked ball, Gold Bay won back service. Above her head, Neeka watched as the flashing red lights of the scoreboard flashed 14-11. They had to win by at least two. If they could manage to steal back service before Gold Bay scored more than two points, they'd have the game.

In the long-winded rally that followed, Gold Bay gained a point when Selina reached for a ball that she should have let go out of bounds. It was an overeager rookie mistake. Then a kill shot added to their score. No longer confident in their win, Neeka swallowed, trying not to panic. She couldn't let the opposing team see her falter. For the fans, her teammates, and herself, she had to remain strong.

But when Gold Bay scored another point, tying the score 14-14, Neeka couldn't help but let her head temporarily drop. If she hadn't remembered that her dad was in the bleachers watching with the rest of her family, Allison, and Brandon, she would have had a harder time lifting it up.

"Come on, girls. The game's not over yet," she yelled to her teammates. "Let's kick Gold Bay out of this party! It's time to celebrate on our own."

But her words weren't enough to keep Hickory Academy from spiking the ball into the net.

It was match point. One more mistake from Hickory Academy, and Gold Bay would be the team heading to State, not them. Neeka wouldn't let that happen. As she prepared to set, she wished on every birthday star in her room that Hickory Academy won. Scratch that, on every star in the sky. There were hundreds of billions upon hundreds of billions up there. Surely one was enough to see them through to State.

Annette passed her the ball and she set it, connecting with it as if it was an extension of her body. In one immaculate swoop, an outside hitter crushed it over the net. Neeka winced, afraid to look but knowing she had to watch.

The spike cleared the net, but the ball was blocked. The front row scrambled to reach it before it touched the floor, but the Hickory Academy girls couldn't reach it in time. It hit the floor, giving Gold Bay the final point they needed to win.

"And we're out," Neeka whispered to herself.

"Oh my God, we made it to Sub-State! Our goal was only to win the District Championships. Look how far you took us. Would you please get up off the floor, Annette," Lacey said, her tone somewhere between a nurturing and scolding.

The minute Hickory Academy had entered the locker room, Annette had literally collapsed face first onto the floor and started bawling loudly. If she wasn't so heartbroken that they were done for the season, Neeka would have laughed. It was pretty ridiculous.

Lacey's words were sincere, but they were all disappointed. No one looked at each other as they sat down, frozen in place, each reluctant to remove their jerseys. The seniors found it particularly hard to move, knowing it would be the last time they ever wore the Hickory Academy colors.

Neeka's mind swept over the final moments of the game. Perhaps if she had set the ball a little higher, the hitter might have been able to deliver a kill shot, an attack that couldn't be blocked. Though she found it immature, she almost didn't blame Annette for crying. They had come so far, but losing still felt awful.

Only one team ends the season at the top of the podium. Everyone else has to lose, she tried to tell the team, but she couldn't form the words. The sounded empty, even in her own ears. Though she felt selfish for thinking so, watching Annette, Neeka made a vow that she would not finish her senior year like this. She would lead the team to State before she graduated, no matter what.

* * * * * * * * * * * * * * * * * *

"If only, if only, if only," Mr. Moore said, echoing Neeka's words at dinner. "If I had a dollar for every time I heard that in the sporting world, I'd be a rich man. Take if from someone who's been there, you can't do that to yourself, little misses. You'll destroy yourself psychologically. Once that happens, you're toast."

Neeka's lip trembled as she listened to Brandon speak, but she refused to cry. "But the hitter I set the ball for could have made a kill shot…"

"No," Mr. Moore said sharply. "No more what ifs. Toughen up or get out. Varsity isn't a place for crybabies."

"Brandon," Donald interjected. "Let her mourn."

"I think Mr. Moore's right," Jamari said. "You didn't see me wailing my eyes out when we lost State."

"Yes you did," Payton and Neeka said together.

"Well, I didn't do it in a restaurant full of people trying to enjoy their chili fries," Jamari retorted, throwing a fry back into its basket.

Why is everyone else in a bad mood? Neeka thought miserably. Only Payton and she had any right to be upset. They'd just ended their season on a depressing note.

It had been Brandon's idea for everyone to go out to dinner, thinking it would help the girls cheer up, but it had turned into a much more solemn occasion. The entire Leigh family was there, but Payton's mom had skipped out on the meal, still unable to sit comfortably next to her future ex-husband.

"It's all my fault," Neeka whimpered.

Payton hugged her. When no one else spoke, she tried to be comforting. "Neeka, every point in the match has to be considered, not just the last. What if Coach Mike had changed up the starting lineup positions before the third set? What if he had sent me in earlier? What if Annette hadn't missed those spikes? What if I hadn't messed up my third serve? If you're going to ask yourself a bunch of what ifs, then ask yourself those. Do not carry all the blame on your shoulders. As Dr. B would say, 'It.is.illogical.'" She tried to do a British accent but somehow sounded like a robot.

Neeka cracked a smile, but only a weak one. She appreciated Payton's efforts, but she couldn't stop obsessing. Not until Payton made her final statement.

"If it wasn't for you, Neeka, we wouldn't have even made it to Sub-State. You didn't bring us down, you gave us wings. Victory wings." Payton glanced over at her dad, who winked. "Anyway, I'm kind of glad we didn't win State this year. I'd rather you be the person to lead us there than Annette. I do feel bad for her. I know she was devastated. But I can't help the way I feel. Give me one good reason you don't think we can make it to State next year."

Neeka considered Payton's words, her mood finally starting to lift. She stared at her burrito, thinking hard. If anything, they'd be better next year. They were losing Annette as *libero*, true. No matter how much they disliked her, there was no denying she was good. But they were also gaining half a JV team that, based on what Neeka had seen, could fare well with a little practice. She could help them the same why she'd help Payton, maybe even arrange a few off-season practices.

"You're right," Neeka said, her mourning period coming to an end. "At State next year, we're going to kick—"

"Renika!" her mom shouted, horrified. "We are in a public place. Mind yourself."

"But, I was going to say butt," she protested.

"I wouldn't have," Jamari said, stealing a bite of his sister's burrito.

CHAPTER 19

Payton felt as if the song *Amazing Grace* should be playing somewhere in the background. Standing in the stuffy corridor a few steps outside Coach Mike's office, she waited with Neeka and Selina as the JV and varsity girls handed in their uniforms. The two teams were crowded in and around his small office as he spoke with the seniors on the team, who were the first to return their jerseys.

"You are the last of the inaugural team," Coach Mike said as the seniors grieved around him. "In three short years, you brought us from being the most inexperienced team on the floor to being the best in not only our district, but our region as well. That is a feat that will live on in the school's history, especially now that we have two shiny trophies to display for not only all the students and faculty to see, but also the volleyball teams that follow in your footsteps. You've set high standards for them to live up to."

He reached into a box and pulled out the Regional trophy. "To honor everything you have done, for helping shape the volleyball program for Hickory Academy so successfully, your names have received a special engraving."

Curious, Payton peeked over everyone's heads. All the varsity team's names were carved into the plaque on the side of the trophy, but Annette and the rest of the senior's name were at the top and written in a more stylish type of calligraphy, one that stood out from the plainer text used for the rest of the names. Payton didn't object. In fact, she found it quite nice. They had, after all, been at the very first match Hickory Academy had ever played.

"Three cheers for the seniors!" Coach Mike said, leading the girls into applause.

Then the office quieted down, turning somber. Payton looked around awkwardly, not really sure what was happening. She wanted to ask Neeka, but she wasn't sure she was allowed to speak. Following the example of the rest of the girls, she stayed silent and watched as Annette and the upperclassman formally handed in their jerseys. It felt like she was standing in the middle of a memorial ceremony.

Unable to keep her tears from falling, Annette hugged her fellow seniors then ran out of the office, waving quickly at Payton and the other two newbies as she hurried up the nearby stairs. Payton felt awful. Graduating from middle school had been easy. She knew what to expect in high school, including what sports were on offer. It must be hard leaving something behind you had no certainty you'd ever be able to get back. College was a lot more competitive than high school.

The three of them eventually made it into the office to hand in their JV and varsity uniforms. They were the last ones left. Everyone else had skipped out as soon as their hands were empty. Suddenly, the remorse they'd witnessed from the seniors hit them. It was hard to make the transition from volleyball back to basketball. They had each grown in unexpected ways during the short season. Payton had learned to work through failure. Neeka discovered the glory and hardship of the spotlight, and Selina... Well, Selina hadn't changed that much, but she was being much more sportsmanlike, though she was still just as competitive as ever.

Coach Mike studied them up and down before accepting their jerseys. "And the newbies become the leaders," he said.

Leaders? Payton questioned. Neeka, yes. But Selina and her? She wasn't sure they deserved that title.

"You're the core of the team, you know that don't you? I wouldn't say you were the most highly skilled girls on the team. Except for you, Neeka. But you have heart. Don't think I didn't notice during the season, no matter how hard I was on you."

Next to her, Neeka stood a little taller. It made Payton smile. *You deserve it, girl.*

Knowing Neeka was destined to be Captain, they'd already talked about her future role on the team. During their first sleepover in ages, Neeka had told her that she planned on being better than Annette, that she wouldn't make the same mistakes Annette had made, like dividing the team or bullying the players. With her eyes cast down, she had also committed herself to not making the same mistake she'd made with Payton. She'd overlooked a teammate in need because she felt threatened.

Payton fully understood why Coach Mike wanted Neeka to be a leader. But her? What could she possibly offer the team?

"I'm telling you this now because I want you to be prepared. Moore, look at me," he instructed.

Payton hadn't realized she'd looked away. She quickly met his gaze. He was serious, but not harshly so. More like a father figure than the Sergeant he had played all season.

"I'm talking to you too, Moore. Did you see the way the fans united behind you? You may not be the best player on the team, but you know how to command an audience. We're nothing without our fans. This team needs you. Promise me I'll see you back on the team next year."

"I promise," Payton said, touched by his words.

"Good. Now also promise me you'll work on your skills until then. You don't want to be a substitute server forever, do you?"

"No, Coach." She shook her head.

"Neeka, I'm counting on you to work with Payton and Selina until then. You have the golden touch. I need them to improve before next year."

"Okay, Coach," Neeka agreed, more than happy to do so.

"I know you're all heading into basketball season. Knowing that's where your origins are and seeing how well you have transitioned from basketball to volleyball, I wish now that I had encouraged all of the other girls to try-out. Have fun, but don't forget about me here in the office while you're off shooting hoops. And for goodness sake, whatever you do, don't injure yourself. In fact, I have no remorse saying it, Neeka, but I'm glad you're only substituting this season. If any of you all see the ball come flying toward you, and you're given the option to risk injury or duck—by all means, duck. Remember, basketball may be your origin, but volleyball is your future. I'm the one who can get you to a State championship."

Only until I make varsity basketball, Payton forecasted, setting a goal to win a State trophy in both sports.

"Listen to me, girls, and listen carefully." Coach Mike leaned in close to them. "I want to win State next year. If we work together, I think we can make it. Are you with me?"

"Yes!" they said in unison.

Watch out, Tennessee, Payton thought. *You haven't seen the last of Hickory Academy.*

ABOUT THE AUTHOR

Pam comes from a long line of volleyball lovers, including her four brothers who all played for their college teams and her father who was a coach. Pam has spent the past two years travelling as a physical therapist with a beach volleyball competition circuit. She figures what better way to semi-retire than to travel from one beach to another, watching the sport she loves. In her spare time she is an avid snorkeler and she loves kayaking and walking the beach with her husband of almost 20 years.